"Danielle Lazarin's *Back* [...] s a
powerful punch—much li [...] its pages.
The stories in this collectio [...] the boundaries of female
desire—not just for sex, but for intimacy, for visibility, for agency.
They talk back to the idea that stories about women are 'domestic,'
burrowing deep to find wildness and a smoldering fury beneath.
The best collection I've read in years, from a phenomenal new
talent."

> —Celeste Ng, *New York Times* bestselling author of
> *Little Fires Everywhere* and *Everything I Never Told You*

"The stories in *Back Talk* are not only fierce and unflinching in
their clear-eyed portrayal of women and girls, they are also tender
and compassionate, imbued with a deep longing; Lazarin's
characters ache for their lives to be without pain. Lazarin is a
sophisticated writer, and her remarkable debut offers us subtle
but profound truths about growing up, moving forward, and
finding ourselves."

> —Edan Lepucki, *New York Times* bestselling
> author of *Woman No. 17* and *California*

"These are wonderful stories—sparkling, witty, and tender, riding
that sweet spot between urbane and vulnerable, between hilarity
and heartbreak, all those impossible contradictions that remind us
of what love is like. Lazarin's astonishing insight and craftsmanship
put me in mind of short-story masters like Ann Beattie and Charles
Baxter. I think she's destined for the big leagues."

> —Dan Chaon, *New York Times* bestselling author of *Ill Will*

"*Back Talk* offers a kaleidoscopic portrait of the contemporary family in a state of creative destruction, flying apart and simultaneously reconstituting itself in new forms. Danielle Lazarin guides us through the varied permutations of her extended, blended families with insightful wit, surpassing empathy, and wry wisdom."

—Peter Ho Davies, author of *The Fortunes*

"Misfits and mess-ups, dreamers and delinquents, kids chafing at adolescence and adults failing at parenthood—it's easy to see yourself in Danielle Lazarin's characters. But these stories, like all good stories, aren't a mirror: they're a window that shows us the whole world."

—Rumaan Alam, author of *Rich and Pretty*

"I absolutely loved this book—from the first page to the last, this collection is stunning for its insight into the lives of young women, revelatory for its finely tuned prose, and unforgettable for its humor and tenderness. I will return to these stories again and again. I envy the reader who gets to discover Danielle Lazarin's work."

—Julie Buntin, author of *Marlena*

"Thank God, a collection of stories about women who don't hate themselves, don't hate other women, don't hate their bodies, don't hate their husbands, or even their ex-husbands, don't hate their sisters, their mothers, their fathers, their children. Women who sometimes choose to have sex and sometimes choose not to. Women who are simply, like me, trying to figure out what it means to be alive, to be in love, to be daughters, parents, siblings, wives, citizens, human beings. I hope Danielle Lazarin writes a million more stories like the ones in *Back Talk* so I can keep reading her work forever."

—Eileen Pollack, author of *A Perfect Life*

Danielle Lazarin's short stories have won grants from the New York Foundation for the Arts and the Northern Manhattan Arts Alliance, the Glimmer Train Family Matters Award, and Hopwood Awards. She is a graduate of the writing programs at Oberlin College and the University of Michigan's Helen Zell Writers' Program. She lives in her native New York City with her husband and daughters.

# BACK TALK

STORIES

Danielle Lazarin

B
BLACKFRIARS

BLACKFRIARS

First published in the United States in 2018 by Penguin Books,
an imprint of Penguin Random House LCC, New York

First published in Great Britain in 2018 by Blackfriars

'Appetite' first appeared in *Colorado Review*; 'Spider Legs' in *Glimmer Train*;
'Window Guards' (as 'Ghost Dog') in *People Holding*; 'The Holographic Soul' in
*Michigan Quarterly Review*; 'Landscape No. 27' in *Indiana Review*; 'Back Talk'
in *Copper Nickel*; 'Dinosaurs' in *Five Chapters*; and 'Gone' in *Boston Review*.

Cover design: Lynn Buckley

A CIP catalogue record for this book
is available from the British Library.

ISBN 978-0-349-13462-8

Printed and bound in Great Britain by
Clays Ltd, St Ives plc

Papers used by Blackfriars are from well-managed forests
and other responsible sources.

This imprint has no connection with The Order of Preachers (Dominicans)

Blackfriars
An imprint of
Little, Brown Book Group
Carmelite House
50 Victoria Embankment
London EC4Y 0DZ

An Hachette UK Company
www.hachette.co.uk

www.littlebrown.co.uk

For my parents

# Contents

*It was different for a girl.*

—*Susan Minot, "Lust"*

# BACK TALK

# Appetite

I n Val's bedroom before Arthur Binder's party, I have one of my black boots on my left foot, and one of my dead mother's shoes—oxblood leather, two-inch heel—on my right. "Which one?" I ask Val.

"The right," she says, "but with the first pair of jeans."

"Yeah?" This is not the first time I've taken the shoes out of my parents' room, but I've never worn them before.

"Yeah, definitely. Those new?"

"New-ish," I say.

At the party, girls say they like my shoes and I say *thank you*; I pretend they are mine.

When Val follows her ex-boyfriend from the living room into a back bedroom, she leaves me on the arm of the chair she was just in, alone with a boy I don't know. He's looking straight at me as he exhales the last of a cigarette through the window screen before extinguishing it in his glass, one of the good ones from the locked part of the liquor cabinet. Because he is beyond handsome, and because he is likely out of my league, I say, "Can I help you?" trying my hardest not to smile.

"I know you," he says, and pats his pockets for another cigarette.

"Oh yeah?" I am still trying to be cute, though he hasn't said this in a flirtatious way.

"You and your friends ran out on the check at my uncles' diner last weekend. You have a cigarette?"

It's true. We were short ten dollars, and somehow it seemed smarter to not leave anything at all. I want to throw up. I also want to kiss him, this boy who clearly doesn't want to kiss me back.

"I don't. My mother died of lung cancer."

"And before she died, she didn't teach you not to steal?"

"Obviously not."

*Come,* my mother used to say when she was particularly frustrated with me, *I want to hurt you, just a little bit,* as she pinched me.

"Had you been boys, we would've come after you. Rich girls," he says, shaking his head.

"I'm not the one in private school."

"Have we met before?"

"Nope." I don't know him, but I recognize his friends; they go to an all-boys private school in the Bronx.

He tells me his name, George, and asks for mine, and then uses it when he offers to refill my empty cup, a plastic one. "Tell me what you want, Claudia," he says, and I feel sweat under the band of my bra at my name in his mouth. While he's in the kitchen, I peel off a twenty from sixty dollars I'm keeping for

Val, who loses things too easily, who has yet to emerge from that back bedroom. I hold it out to him when he hands me my drink. "This is all I have, but give it to your uncles."

Our fingers graze as he takes it. He thanks me. The diner, he explains, is the last of its kind in New York. "People like to eat shit out of trucks now," he says.

At half past twelve George asks if I am staying much longer. I look at the door where Val is with her now-not ex. The last thing I want is to be stuck on a late-night subway platform with the two of them, as they paw at each other or rehash their last breakup. I find Val's jacket in a pile in the bedroom and zip her two remaining twenties into a pocket.

Once outside, George asks, "Which way?"

"The A."

"Me too," he says, but already I don't believe him.

George rides with me to my stop, the last one. He walks the five blocks to my building as if he knows where he is going. When I ask him where he lives, he points downtown and east. "Oh, that way," I tease him. "Yes, precisely," he replies.

He takes the step below mine outside my building, asks, "Is your mother really dead?"

"I'm wearing her shoes," I say, and we both look down at my feet.

"Doesn't prove anything."

"I may be a thief, but I'm not a liar."

"We'll see."

"Will we?" I ask, when I want to ask why he hasn't kissed

me, when he does, with one hand on my waist, which he uses to push me gently toward the building when he's done. On the train he put his number in my phone but won't take mine. "You'll call," he assures me, shooing me up the steps. He doesn't move from his step until I am through both sets of locked doors and safely in the lobby.

Our building used to be grand, sixty years ago. Now the floor dips right before the elevator, worn down by years of impatient waiting. The mosaic around the mailboxes needs cleaning and repair; the crests of its ocean waves, though we live nowhere near the ocean, swell no more. Tiles fall off every month; the super slips them into his pocket with a headshake. When I was a child, I'd work them like loose teeth. "Stop that," my father would say while flipping through the mail, and I would put my hands at my sides, my fingers itching to finish the work. Back then, Josef was our super; he'd cup my chin every time I brought him a tile, as though I were bringing him gold coins. When Josef moved upstate to live near his grandkids, we got a new super. He's good at fixing plumbing, but he doesn't talk much; he doesn't smile at the kids, though I guess I am not a kid anymore. A few upscale restaurants have moved in; more strollers, nicer ones, take up the sidewalks, the steps to the subway station, but our building seems to be falling down despite this, despite all the people who show up in our neighborhood with their money and their dreams and their ripe uteruses. Somewhere in the building's basement, there is a collection of tiles big enough to construct a new ocean.

The elevator smells of my neighbors' sins: takeout, trash, too much perfume. In my fifteen years, I've ridden with them all: the pot dealer in 8C; Mr. Rivera, his crumpled receipts falling from his jacket pockets; dirty boots and hangovers; and my parents, who gathered themselves in a steely silence after a fight, before they entered the world pretending to be happier than they were. Tonight, I am grateful to ride alone, to not have anyone know I am coming home this late.

Off the elevator, I slide out of the shoes, rest for a moment barefoot on the cool floors of the hallway. It's not the heel that bothers me, but the toes; they pinch. I only remember my mother wearing the shoes twice: to a cousin's bar mitzvah, and to a dinner with my grandparents. Both times she ended the evening in stockinged feet. The shoes are at least twenty years old but it's as though no one has worn them, and I count on this when I return them to my parents' closet in the morning, while my father is buying the paper. I'm not sure Dad even knows they're there anymore, that he can remember what we've kept of hers and what we've thrown out. The only evidence is the slight ache I have in my arches the next day, a secret he's not interested in discovering.

I was twelve when my mother died. It took three years. Before she left, we let her have as much anger and fear as she wanted, even as it suffocated the rest of us.

My older sister, Michelle, asked once to go to boarding school.

"You only have a little more than a year to go," Dad reminded her.

"I just want out of here," she whimpered across the kitchen table, and my mother gave a little moan from the other room as if to say she was on her side. Then Mich leaned over her baked ziti and cried. I remember thinking how selfish she was; I thought she was crying because Dad had said no. He returned to his dinner, wiping his mustache between bites.

Seven months after my mother's death, Mich left for college. Last spring break, her sophomore year, while everyone else her age was getting tan and wasted on beaches in the southern United States, Mich came home. It felt foolish to even utter the word *spring* in New York; moisture still dripped, cold, from the heating pipe in the bathroom, from our noses. It had been a miserable winter. The snow fell regularly but wouldn't stick. The sidewalks were slicked with a sheet of ice so thin we walked with our feet clenched for months.

I'd imagined Mich coming home with interesting friends and stories, with music I'd never heard of, but most of our conversations were her clucking at me, her tone dripping with the kind of pity I'd been trying to shake now that I was finally in high school, now that fewer people knew the big horrible thing that had happened to us. But instead, college had made her more serious than she already was. She either dismissed her classmates for their ignorance about "real-world problems" or droned on endlessly about her course work, always circling back to impending world collapse, alternately due to population explosion, political implosion, or the general stupidity of humanity.

During that break, she insisted we sit down for dinner every night, as though we had ever done this. One night she made us roasted chicken and potatoes, with two kinds of greens she'd taken the train all the way to the market at Union Square to get.

As soon as we sat, she started talking, and I was eating because in truth, it had been a while since we'd had food that good. Dad was too consumed by his chicken to even nod along to Mich's chatter like he usually did. They both had bottles of beer at the top of their plates, and I could tell he was relaxed, happy to have her home.

The whole time she talked she was shaking salt onto her potatoes and it was as though she was unaware she was doing it, a zombie's hand at work. I waited for her to take her first bite and be shocked by the snowcap of salt she was amassing on the world's smallest pile of mashed potatoes, but she forgot to do that, too.

"I think I'm just going to stay home," she said. "I don't think college is for me. Not now."

My father put his fork down and reached out to touch her shoulder. And for the twentieth time in my recent memory, Mich cried in her food at our table.

I took more mashed potatoes, because it was clear no one else had the stomach for them. There was a time, my father says, when I didn't eat, when I refused to sit at a table for more than a few minutes, the world far more interesting than food. I don't remember that. I'm not one of those girls. I have an appetite.

The morning after I meet George, I hear my father on the phone, early, before he's started the coffee. When I come out to the kitchen, he's leaning against the counter, phone in his hand, hair askew. "Come downstairs with me?" he asks. "Your sister's here."

Back in New York, Mich found a boyfriend, someone she had gone to high school with who she'd always had a thing for. She moved in with him in Queens over the summer, and my father and I got our quiet back. When she comes uptown to see us now, she's a touch lighter than she was when she was at school. As we wait on the same steps I was on with George hours earlier, I ask my father if that's over now, too, if John broke up with Mich.

"She didn't say, exactly. I don't really know."

"Okay," I say, not asking him what he didn't ask her.

"And weren't you staying at Val's last night?" my father asks.

"Changed my mind."

"Just let me know next time, will ya?"

"It was late. I didn't want to wake you."

"Just send a text," he says, but doesn't ask how I got home, who took me home.

A few minutes later, John's car is idling at the curb. My sister slams her door and starts unloading blankets from the backseat into my father's arms. Dad's glaring at John, who stares out the front windshield as though none of us are there. Dad wants to drop the blankets and be that father, the one who gets in the face of his daughter's shitty boyfriend, but he's too busy being the father holding the pile of blankets.

"Some help here, Claudia," Mich says. Her voice is hoarse, her cheeks flushed.

"What, your arms don't work?" I say to John through the small opening of the passenger's side window. When I close the trunk, he drives away.

The three of us wait for the elevator, our arms full. No one wants to be the one to say it, but after a few minutes it's clear the elevator is broken. Dad starts up the stairs with his load and Mich and I follow. We haul each box, each garbage bag stuffed with clothes, up the five flights silently, until we are done.

There's a spare bedroom, but it's the one Mom died in, the one that was mine before the cancer came, the one we all pretend isn't there. Mich drops a bag on the bed opposite mine, into the mess of my schoolwork and discarded outfits.

"I'll move it later," she tells me.

"It's okay," I say. "We'll figure it out."

The first place George takes me is the diner. We're walking around Midtown one afternoon the following week, and he asks me if I'm hungry and I say yes. It's so different in the daylight, I don't realize where we are till his uncles are around us, kissing him on both cheeks. They call him Georgie and wink at him while looking me over. They do not seem to share his memory of the night I was last here.

"It's okay," he says as he takes my coat and hangs it on a hook between the bathrooms. He directs me to a stool at the end of the counter; he fills a cup with water for me. Through the window that leads to the kitchen, George says something to the cooks in broken Spanish. They wave him in, and he tells me to sit tight. I watch him push up the sleeves of his shirt and cook, the gentle way he moves the eggs around the griddle, his long eyelashes, the curves of his muscles under his T-shirt. Plate in hand, he motions toward an empty booth. George sits next to me while I eat, chewing ice cubes from his soda cup, taking bites of my omelet without asking. As his extended family rushes around us, looking sideways at the kitchen while they take orders, at us, George lifts my free hand and kisses the back of it. "Good?" he asks about the eggs.

"So good," I say. "Thank you."

Before we leave, he buses the table, not letting me help. This is how the next eight months will go: George won't ask me what I want but he will give me what I need. Here I am, being a kind of girl I swore I'd never be, but it's just for a little while, and I like letting him handle it, every time he tells me something is okay even when it's not.

The dog in the apartment next door howls. We can't ever figure out why—it's not sirens, or doorbells, or fighting neighbors. One evening, I find Mich in the kitchen, listening.

"So sad," she says, and gestures to the wall with a half-peeled carrot.

"You've never noticed that?"

She shakes her head.

"He's been doing that for years."

She returns to her pile of vegetables. This is how my sister is all the time now, her hands on some long-ignored kitchen tool, or flipping through one of my parents' old cookbooks, its pages so unused I can hear the spine cracking as she presses her weight into the book. She wears an apron more than she wears shoes, only leaving for her job at the library or grocery shopping. She turns her phone off for days. The battery drains, and when she recharges it, there are messages from her friends, whom she waits weeks to call back. She's never been better, I hear her tell them, another lie in our house.

The last time we went to the store together, she popped an old CD of my mother's, Nina Simone, into the car stereo. "I love this song," she said when "Ne Me Quitte Pas" came on, raising the volume. "Listen," she said to me, and I let her translate each lyric for me, even though I take French. She got through the part where Simone sings about being her lover's shadow: of the shadow itself, of his hand, of the goddamn dog. Her voice cracked on this last one. "Ugh, it's so fucking beautiful I can't stand it," she said. "Right?" She smiled, but in that sad way of hers.

There was a time when I would have argued with her, or at least laughed at her intensity, but I like coming home to find her in the kitchen; I like eating her food, sitting with her while she makes it.

"Whoa," I said, and she took this as agreement.

Today, I take my usual spot on the other side of the island where she's working.

"Shit. It's five thirty already?" Mich asks, pushing a strand of still-wet hair out of her face. She gets clean for cooking the way other people would for dates or jobs, so at least there's that.

"Five thirty-two," I tell her, reading the time from my phone, where there are no messages from George. He'd rather see me, he says. I think of watching him come around the corner toward me earlier this afternoon, how his steps quickened when he spotted me.

"Where were you all this time?"

"The park."

"Inwood?"

"Central."

"With George," she says, a conclusion.

"Yes."

Mich purses her lips before igniting a burner. "He's taking up a lot of your time."

"He's not taking it. I am giving it to him."

She pours oil in a pot. Her hand still on the bottle, she asks, "Have you?"

"Not yet," I say.

"Well, be careful," she says.

"Yes, I know, condoms and all that."

"Well, yeah, but that's not what I meant." She shakes her head. "Can you grab me a clean dish towel?"

I find one in the drawer next to the sink. My mother's mind, efficient till nearly the end, is still at work in our kitchen, even if she rarely used it to cook, not like this. Mich pours me a glass of wine from the bottle she's cooking with. When she hands it to me, I can smell herbs on her fingertips. She says, "But that's it," though I haven't even asked for any.

She bangs a wooden spoon against the top of the pot, shaking off bits of onion. "You should invite him for dinner."

"Why?"

"I want to meet him."

"Yes, but does Dad?"

"Dad just wants us to be happy, that's all."

I picture George at our table, the way he spreads his elbows when he eats. He'd sit in the chair my mother used to sit in, next to my father, because that's the only one left. Would doing so cause Mich to cry into her food again? Just last night I caught her looking at pictures of John online, with new girlfriends, perhaps. He is leaning into the laps of so many different girls in these photos, it's hard to tell if he's committed to any one of them in particular.

"I don't care," she said. "I just want to know." She had a glass of wine in one hand, the rest of the bottle on the windowsill next to her bed. Dad buys these for her, too.

"It would be okay if you did care," I said.

"But I don't. I just want to see again that he's a douchebag."

"He is."

She nodded her assent but kept clicking.

"It isn't worse, right?" I ask in the kitchen, after a few sips of wine have made us both comfortable. "A love heartbreak, over what we went through with Mom?"

She rolls her eyes. "That's stupid. You don't even know how stupid that is," she says.

"How could that feel worse? I don't understand."

"Not worse, but, well, you don't understand. It's just . . ."

"Fuck."

"Yes, fuck," she says, and stirs her soup.

One Friday morning Val and I are on the same bus to school. She stands above me, her hip against the pole. Her earbuds dangle from her hands, as though she is thinking of putting them back in.

"You going tonight, to that party on the East Side?" I ask her.

"I don't know yet," she says, the start of a string of maybes till, by spring, she'll barely be talking to me at all. She scrunches up her pale face before she says, "You think it's a good idea to bring George?"

The week before, George, a little drunk, forcefully removed the arm of one of our friends from my shoulder. The friend said he was bruised, but he's a known exaggerator.

"He goes to an all-boys school; he doesn't get it," I say. And then, "George is the nicest guy I've ever met."

"To you, maybe."

When we get off the bus I start up the stairs without her; I'm late for French. I overslept this morning; Mich must have turned off my alarm, and though I'm planning to be furious with her for it, midway through class I reach into my bag for my workbook to find she packed me a lunch. Today it's a stack of handmade summer rolls, pomegranate seeds, and a hunk of cheddar she made me promise not to tell Dad the price per pound of, each in its own container, and a five-dollar bill, her backup plan, folded in thirds at the bottom of the brown paper bag. I eat in a corner of the library, hiding the bag behind a physics textbook, alone and happy about it.

That night, I go with George to the party. On the train uptown afterward, I lay my legs across his lap. We make jokes about the couple standing by the doors fighting, a pair of earbuds stringing them together. We think we won't ever be them; we can't possibly. Mostly, though, we ride in silence—a good silence, not like the one Val gave me at the party, not like the one that settles over the dinner table at home after we've run out of things to say about the food Mich has made.

I drank too much at the party. We get off a stop early so I can get some air. We walk along Seaman Avenue, Inwood Hill Park dark and empty next to us. Tipsy, I think the puddles of smashed car windows on the sidewalk are works of art. So many little pieces to reflect the streetlights, and I want to get closer, and I do, and then George's arm is across my ribs, holding me up.

"Hey," he says. "You'll hurt yourself." He waltzes me away from the glass to a bench. He sits next to me.

When he pulls out a cigarette, he apologizes. He always does.

"I don't care," I say. "Really. It's not like I'm going to marry you and you'll die on me like my mom did."

"Whoa."

"I'm joking."

"Which part?"

"Um, all of it."

"You are going to marry me, then?"

When I turn to look at him, George is staring back at me as though he wouldn't be afraid if I said yes, even if I meant it. No man has ever looked at me so fearlessly, not even my own father.

"Smoking had nothing to do with it," I tell him. Then, I still believed my mother had stopped smoking before either of us was born. I didn't know that she'd walk to the park after Mich and I had gone to bed, sit on a bench like the one we are sitting on now. Then, this belief mattered.

"I didn't mean that, to upset you." He puts his hand on my knee.

I take his half-smoked cigarette from his fingers, stealing a drag before I stub it out under my boot. I climb onto his lap and draw my legs around him, kissing the bones around his eyes, his jaw. Underneath his coat, I find his belt buckle.

"Not here," he says, and takes my hands out.

When we are pressed against each other somewhere—at parties; lately, midday at my apartment—the only thing George will say about it is "No rush." He says it into my ear, with that sweet smile of his, and even though I will say to him that I'm fine, that I want to keep going, he is the one who stops us. Maybe he is afraid of me after all.

On the bench, I whisper to him, "No one is here. No one is watching."

He laughs, says, "Someone is always watching," before giving my longest finger one hard suck, before he convinces me it's time to go home.

One Tuesday I cut pre-calc to meet George. Mich is at work; I check her shifts, which she puts on a calendar she's bought in the kitchen. Her life is the only one on it. The elevator is broken again, but I make it up the stairs without seeing any neighbors. I drop my backpack and jacket by the front door, which I leave unlocked for George, as he knows it will be, as he knows to lock it behind him. I'm early, and I have to pee. I walk past my father's bedroom, the door to which is open, which is odd; he shuts it every morning, though Mich tells him it's better to air the apartment out, and she'll crack the windows till we have a nice draft going that no one wants either. She must have opened the door before she left. When I go to shut it, I see them: two sets of soles, a mass arching the blanket that's always folded at the end of the bed. Just feet, but it's enough. They don't hear me. He won't know, but I'll know, always.

I grab my things and shut the door, push the elevator

button, forgetting. I get down the stairs as fast as I can in socks. I run into George on the third floor.

I have to sit down; I can't even make it to the next landing. I put my head on my knees and breathe. A school social worker taught me this in sixth grade, when I thought I was having a panic attack. My mother wasn't even dead yet, but I practiced it, because I knew I would need it one day.

George rubs my spine. "Hey," he says. "What's going on?"

"My dad is fucking some woman in our apartment," I say from between my knees.

"Come," he says, taking my shoes from me and undoing the knots. "Let's go." He slides them on my feet, ties the laces again. We go out the front door of my building together, quickly, but George holds my hand, makes it seem like we're in no rush at all.

On Sunday Dad and I are in the car, the trunk full of groceries. He is whistling, though the radio is tuned to a talk station. It is one of those moist winter days when you could be tricked into believing spring will be here soon, except for the gritty piles of snow that sit at the edges of the sidewalks, for the fact that the calendar is just over the hump of March. At the supermarket, we followed the pattern we've fallen into when shopping for Mich: my father steering the cart, calling out the contents of the list to me. He doesn't like reading the boxes, and he is easily confused by the various green leaves of herbs, so I bring the items to the cart, which he still fills with what we've always eaten: the same shape of pasta, rotisserie chicken, presliced cheese, things Mich rolls her eyes at when she puts them away. Every week, as my father watches her items move across the scanner, he mumbles, "Cheaper than therapy," and half-grimaces.

I spent the past few days recalling to George the odd hair clips or new kinds of pens that have surfaced on the coffee table, the multiple confirmations of my spending the night out every now and then, and these kinds of moods—whistling and an unfamiliar lightness—that overtake my father so rarely I don't want to ruin them by asking where they come from.

"What if he marries her?" I said to George.

He shook his head. "He won't," he said, but I thought of my father reciting the mourner's kaddish at my mother's funeral when I'd never heard him utter a prayer, of all the things I don't know about him.

Dad takes the Dyckman exit off the highway, and as we take the hard left onto Henshaw, the CD, the Nina Simone, starts playing. The car does this sometimes; no one cares to get it fixed, but usually one of us switches back to the radio or shuts the CD off. Neither of us does that today. It's in the middle of that song, the one that Mich played for me.

"What language did you take in high school?" I ask him.

"Latin."

"Useful," I say, trying to be sarcastic, but when I'm nervous everything I say is monotone and even, and he misses my joke.

"Not really," he says.

"I'm worried about Mich," I say, in the same tone.

"What about?" he asks, his eyes on the road.

"She seems . . ." I search for the right word, but the best I can do is "bad."

"You mean about John? That's just a little heartache. She'll be fine." He goes back to whistling; the track has switched to something that's more in line with his birdsong, and he picks it up.

Of course he believes this, because what is love in my family if not inked in suffering? Mich crying in her bed in the mornings before she thinks I'm awake, the line of women who leave my father by various means—cancer, growing up—the girlfriends who will never last more than half a year at best, or who he'll push away (I'll never know; I'll never be kind enough to ask). Even my mother's favorite stories were about the outrageous fights of our downstairs neighbors, all the words and shattering objects we were privy to. "It was like a war," she'd say, gleefully. *Ne me quitte pas,* everyone in my family sings, happy to hear about suffering, willing to be the shadow of someone's dog. But I am not yet sixteen, and I am still afraid of pain—for myself, for all of us.

I shut off the music. "I know about your girlfriend," I say.

"She's not my girlfriend. Not that that is your business."

"Whatever. I saw her on Tuesday, at the apartment."

"And why weren't you in school?"

I don't answer. I didn't plan to mention the woman; I didn't plan to have to explain myself.

"Claudia. Why were you home?" he asks again.

"I was meeting George."

We turn onto our block. All the questions that follow cross his face. He pulls a U-turn up to the hydrant by the side entrance of the building. He pops the trunk of the car but doesn't unlatch his seatbelt.

"Get the groceries."

"God, don't you see it? Don't you see anything anymore?" I ask.

I sit in the front seat, waiting for an answer, or a punishment, as he gets out of the car and starts lifting the bags out. Then he opens my door for me. He's gone before I can get the bags in my hands.

Upstairs, Mich is working on her latest obsession, some historic pasta sauce she found in a book. Yesterday, she went to three different shops on Arthur Avenue for the ingredients. I drop the bags at her feet. "What's wrong with you?" she asks. Her face falls into a reflection of mine, sour. I wonder if we still look alike, the way we did during that brief period of time when we only wanted to be with each other, and suctioned ourselves to one another's bodies on the street, on the subway. Mich went to middle school and that stopped, along with people commenting on our resemblance. "You look sick."

"Yeah. I'm not feeling well," I say, and go into the bathroom.

"Dad parking?" she calls out after me.

I don't answer.

"Claude?"

I strip out of my clothes and get into a hot shower, where I can cry in peace. Mich comes and knocks on the door but that, too, I pretend I don't hear.

Dad comes home with two bottles of wine, whistling again, but he isn't talking to me. It's muggy in the apartment, and the long cooking of sausages and tomatoes only makes it more so. I pour myself a glass of wine. Both Dad and Mich notice it, but neither says anything. They talk about the markets on Arthur Avenue, how much they've stayed the same since Dad was a kid, how his father, an otherwise observant Jew, once brought home a pork sausage and his mother lost it on him. My father eats with gusto, even though tomato sauce gives him heartburn, even though there are beads of sweat on his brow. Halfway through dinner he stands to take off his shirt, tossing it onto an empty chair. He finishes the meal in his undershirt, a white V-neck that barely conceals his hairy chest. "It's good," he says to her, and she says she's glad he likes it.

Dad offers to do the dishes, and I go straight to my room. "You feeling better?" Mich asks when she comes in a little later. She takes her socks off, puts them in the hamper.

"Not really."

"You need anything?"

"No," I mumble into my pillow.

I listen to her undressing, zippers and the pull of a brush through her hair. She says, "Look, they're never gonna be who you think they are. It's better to start lowering your expectations now. It's the only way to be happy."

I want to tell her it's not George, that it's Dad, that it's a woman who will always be a stranger to us, that I am scared I'll never remember our mother correctly, but I'm so afraid of breaking Mich's heart any further that I don't, not that night, not ever. I pull my blanket up over my chin and say good night.

I invite George to dinner in the same breath I tell him about the fight with my father. We're walking out of a movie. Outside, the late winter wind has returned like those muggy days never happened. It hits me in the chest, but George puts his arm around my shoulders.

"Ah, I don't know if that's the best idea," he says.

"He'll like you," I say.

"No," he says, "he will not."

He's right. No matter how polite George is, my father will sniff out his cigarettes, how easily I take his lead.

"So what?" I say. "Fuck him."

"That's your dad, Claudia. Respect him."

"Are you kidding me?"

"You've only got one parent left. Don't fuck it up, and don't use me to do it." His arm is still firmly around my shoulders. George was always kind to me, even when he wasn't being gentle.

At the corner I stick my hand up for a cab as though I have the money. It's a long ride, all the way west, uptown. Someone will be up; someone will pay for it. They will be upset, but they will do it.

"What are you doing?" George asks me.

"Going home. Alone."

"Okay," he says, and kisses my cheek as a cab pulls up.

By the time we hit the West Side Highway, the Hudson black out my window, all I can see is George as he held the cab door open for me, him letting me go. The cab takes the curves of the outline of Manhattan, and I concentrate on the sound of wheels going over the highway like the gallops of a large horse. Uptown, nothing glitters at you. Mostly what you see is New Jersey, not a rising skyline, not the possibilities of all the lives waiting to cross your path. You try not to look back when you head in this direction.

Mich is waiting outside the building, welcoming my heartbreak home with a credit card she hands me through the cab's window. When I get out of the car she puts her arm around me, asks if I am okay.

"I just want to go to bed," I say.

"I know," she answers.


"I'll come," George says. We're lying on my bed on our stomachs, watching the rain hit the windows.

"Invitation rescinded," I say.

It's predictable, how my saying no to him ignites a hunger for me, the way it makes him behave more like a teenage boy than ever before, as if he is remembering in one fell swoop all the yeses I've given to him before this no, the foolishness of his insistence that we be so sure, leave no room for doubt. He leans on his elbow, starts to rub my back. All of our clothes are off within minutes. I get what I want, and when it's over he recovers everything he has tossed to the floor as he undressed me: each sock and T-shirt layer; he turns my jeans the right way around before he hands them to me.

In New York, everyone wants to lay claim to a piece of something. They write on the walls of the subway tunnels, where it's dark and wet and full of rats. They stay long enough to write poems. I lay claim to George for a little while, and then I let him go because I think it's good practice for the rest of my life, because I think the longer you love someone the more it hurts, the more you have to imagine them in places they'll never be again. I thought at some point in my life I'd stop having those dreams about my mother, dreams so stupid and small they could be memories, but they're not: her sitting in the passenger's seat of the car, or locking the front door, then checking her coat pocket for her wallet. I thought I understood a way around loss. I wait a month before I tell George we shouldn't be together anymore, before his breath on any part of my body stops making me crazy with desire, before I say that it hurts me more than it hurts him, because I need to believe that's true. For years, I'll picture him where he no longer is: the maroon sweater he folds, the school insignia faceup, and leaves on Mich's bed, the gentle way he closes a door; I'll fill the apartment with more ghosts.

On the evening after I have sex with George, I come home to Mich and Dad standing over three trash bags in the living room. Mom's clothes are draped over the couch; the plastic hangers she so hated litter the rug in a messy stack. We've tried to clean out Mom's room before, but it hasn't ever been enough. I touch a dress over the easy chair. I want to remember her wearing it, but I can't. There is a small pile on the end of the couch where I usually sit. Things for someone—it's not clear who—to keep. The clothes don't even smell like anything except our house, and that is a smell I won't recognize till I've moved out, years later, when Dad mails me a jacket I left in the apartment by mistake.

"What can I do?" I ask, though I do not want to do anything.

Mich hands me a box of jewelry. "Pick out anything that looks nice." She examines the bottom of a pair of shoes to see how worn they are. I look at her, but she isn't looking back. "Or that you want," she adds.

After a few minutes, I put the jewelry in my hands back into the box. Play stuff, my mother would say. It doesn't remind me of her, but still.

"I'm going to order a pizza," I say. I am starving.

"I was going to make us cod," Mich says.

"Pizza's great," Dad says. "Then you can both help. We can get it done, once and for all."

I can't, but Mich does. She saves me a few things—a pair of earrings my mother wore as a girl, a couple of dresses I am still not the right size for, whose shoulders bear the bumps of crappy hangers, untouched for too long. The shoes are nowhere. Maybe I should have asked for them, but I didn't.

It's summer and I'm at the park, walking a dog Mich says we are just fostering but that she'll try and convince my father, unsuccessfully, to keep, till she moves out again, deciding that a life with a dog is a fine substitution for the company of a man, for us. The dog's name is Taco. He's small and scrappy and always sticking his snout along the baseboards, making me paranoid we have mice. Still, I like having a reason to get out, to separate the chunks of time between my babysitting jobs, walking kids home from camp and cutting up apples for them, and shopping runs for Mich.

I take Taco out to the edge of the peninsula, where even on a muggy day like today you can still find a breeze. Under the trees, the ground is dirt dry, littered with bottle caps and ribbons from balloons from birthday parties, two of which are in full swing around me. I'm pouring water into my palm for Taco, feeling a bit crazy for doing so, when I hear the whoops of the boys up on C-Rock. All summer long they jump from the cliff edge, scaling who knows what just for a chance to plunge into a dirty river with a current that could kill any one of them. Today, must be five boys up on those rocks. Bare chested, T-shirts tucked into the back pockets of their shorts. I know George has done it, not with the boys he goes to school with, but the ones he's known since he was young, before private school. When he first told me, I refused to believe him. When I understood he was serious I asked, "Isn't it cold? And dangerous? You could die."

"Nah, it feels good. It's beautiful."

We were on the roof of a building down the block from me, where one of his cousins was a super. When the metal door closed behind us I felt like we were going to be locked out up there, in a place we weren't supposed to be. And then I turned around to see the view. The last bend of the Harlem River. The other rooftops, empty. And George, freshly showered, grinning ear-to-ear, as though he'd built every one of the things before us, laid each brick, cut the pathway for the canal, made the leaves of spring begin to bud. He was wearing a clean white T-shirt, a nice pair of jeans; the breeze was warm. He'd brought a blanket, a bottle of wine.

I turned to look at C-Rock, the river below, how little shore there was beneath. I didn't know which part of it he thought the beauty was in—the proximity to death, the feel of the freezing water rising to meet you on a hot summer day—but I didn't want to picture him doing it. I covered my eyes. "Let's not talk about it anymore, okay?"

"Okay," he said, and took my hands off my eyes, placed them around his waist. Over his shoulder, I watched a lone yellow cab try to find its way out of a tangle of one-way streets, like a fish separated from its school, desperate and hungry and alone.

On the peninsula, Taco crawls under the bench, where there's shade. And then I see George, next in line. I don't know if it's him, actually. It looks like him to me, how he holds his body, or in this case, doesn't—no hands over his knees, not fetal and scared like the kid who went before, who yelped like a kicked puppy. This boy's arms are out to the world. No screaming, just falling.

# Floor Plans

When Lev says "things" he means our marriage, and when he says "fail" he means a decision he has already made without me. When he says this, both of us are looking out the living room window at the neighbors having a piano delivered, piece by piece, through their window three floors below ours.

"We're young," he says by way of consolation.

"We are?" I lean on my wrists, bored of watching the piano's precarious journey, but not wanting to leave Lev alone, even as standing beside him makes me angry. Neither of us feels young. Not old, either, but old enough to know we'll pay for these choices, the one over a decade ago, the one today. I don't want it to be true, for our marriage to be so easy to let go of, but I sense he is right. I understand him, after all, my practical, fair husband who suggests we split everything fifty-fifty, including the apartment that we both want to stay in but will have to sell, even though his parents provided the down payment, even though it is Lev's job that pays most of the mortgage. If divorce can't ever be easy, we can aim for quicker, kinder, cleaner than what it could be. No raised voices, no shame, no going back.

Lev has moles, handsome ones, on his cheek. The morning after we agree to divorce, I study them, deciding to miss them, these marks I first found a distraction. He needs more sleep than I do, and usually I am out of bed before he is, but this morning I linger because it's the end, the last time we share a bed, a room. I don't touch him. When I've had my fill of looking at him, I pick up his wedding ring from his nightstand, next to his watch and two bills folded into thirds, and slide it on my thumb, the only finger it fits on, loosely. He doesn't wake up. I can't remember if he always did that, slept without it, or if this is the start of relieving himself of me. I am wearing one of his T-shirts; every night, I pick one up from the floor where he drops them. I wonder what I will sleep in once we are apart.

When I tell people about the divorce, their faces fall. They say something kind about him, wait for me to contradict it, but I don't disagree, usually, even if I don't want to hear it. My friends like him. He is likable, lovable. Some of these same friends say they are giving us space, by which they mean they are taking space from our messiness, afraid it will rub off on them, afraid that if we can fall apart, they can, too, even if they aren't married or even in love, even if they loved one of us more than the other all along. They're afraid of the questions they might start asking, the questions I barely want to ask now that I have to, the ones that Lev has been asking himself, but not me, apparently, for months: How much and for how long and why?

Someone asks if we tried counseling. Talking our way out. Fucking our way out. Vacationing or center-locating or finding a way out that isn't out. I stop telling people. They find out anyway—they call; they e-mail; they send vague, useless text messages. *How are you? Let me know what you need. At least,* begins a hundred sentences, not one of which makes me feel any better. They take sides, though we don't think there are sides to take. Mutual, mutual. The whole world splits.

Two weeks later I watch boxes—Lev, sending his files to his brother's house in Connecticut, as though this is what I am after, evidence of twenty years of half-finished book ideas—being carried out the front door by two men who seem impossibly young and I wonder how many people's lives they dismantle on a daily basis.

While they work, I clean the fridge of everything I do not like to eat that Lev does: bottled salad dressings, olives, tubs of cream cheese. When I take the containers to the trash compactor next to the elevator, there is Juliet, from 7H.

"Redoing the floors?" she asks. She puts a hand on her belly, and though it is flat, I know what that means.

"Separating," I say, because I can't bring myself to say "divorce."

She cringes, moves her hand over her heart. "I'm so sorry," she whispers, and then waits for me to respond. I nod at her, reluctant to express gratitude, even as I know it is the right thing to do. I wait for her to look for her keys, or for the movers to need something from me, but we stand there, my door wedged open with a folded cereal box, her eyes taking a quick accounting of the light that comes through the kitchen window. She moves her hand to her own door, which is unlocked already. I stand by the compactor, waiting for her to move.

"Well, let me know if there's anything I can do," she says before she goes inside.

Later, the apartment seeming no bigger absent Lev's things— he barely took any furniture, leaving behind everything nice for staging purposes—I remember that 7H is a one-bedroom.

Within a week, we have an offer in our hands. In the handwritten letter they slide under the door, they address us both formally, as though we are ancient. Lev and I have been in the building for five years longer than they have, for sure, but there can't be more than a few years between us. I work in landscaping, and I come home tracking mud. I wear dresses on the weekends, but my skin won't recover from the sun; no amount of polish will hide the dirt under my nails.

They don't mention the divorce. It's clear they want to combine the apartments, to merge all the energy of a marriage that works, that is making things, to wash out the faultiness of ours. A *once-in-a-lifetime-opportunity*, they write in the letter, a restrained begging.

"We didn't even have to die for their dream," I say to Lev when I get him on the phone at his new apartment, a sublet he moved into not a week after we decided to go through with the split. He called the timing lucky. I sniff for someone else.

"That's a good offer," he says. I can hear him opening a drawer, the clang of silverware.

"We can get more," I say. My half of the apartment sale is all I'll have when we're done.

"I don't know," he says, and pauses. "There's no broker this way. If we put it on, it's just so much hassle."

"From them. We can get more from them."

I hear him chewing on the other end of the line. It's nearly eleven; he must be working if he's eating this late.

"What makes you say that?" he asks when he's done with his bite.

I think of Juliet's hand on her abdomen, the ache she seemed to feel over the end of my marriage, a brand of sympathy, since all of this started, I've been working hard to shut out. Lev has always been practical. Before we bought our place, he made multiple spreadsheets; he wouldn't let me say I loved any of the apartments we saw, because he thought it made the choice cloudy. I had always thought the clean workings of his mind were good to have on my side.

We'd been dating for less than three months when he said to me, "I could totally marry you." By then I understood him enough to know that he wouldn't have said as much if he didn't mean it. "Yes," I said.

"I wasn't asking," he said.

"I am," I said back.

On the phone now, I tell him, "There's real money there," with the same false confidence I did that night a decade ago.

"You're sure?"

"Do you trust me or not?"

"Robin." He says my name sharply, as though I have no

reason to ask that question, as though I am the one who disappointed him. "Of course." He takes another bite of whatever he's eating. "One round," he says.

"Okay," I say, knowing it will take more, but that it will be easy to hide the negotiating from him till we get what we want.

I don't tell Lev about Juliet's pregnancy, or about how we are becoming friends, about the nights when her husband is working late or is away and I go over to watch television, which we end up muting, talking about our childhood pets and who we were in high school, our legs careful not to touch on her couch. "I always thought I'd be a journalist," she says one night. Two days before, we countered their offer by 10 percent.

"That's what Lev does."

"Oh yeah? Does he like it?"

"I think so. I mean, the money's crappy," I say, trying to make her feel better, but she shakes her head indignantly.

"Yeah, but there's more to it than money," she says.

James, her husband, is some kind of banker. This explains the suits, the grimness that is mostly awkward and that I have to believe, for Juliet's sake, conceals someone kind. Everything in their apartment is gorgeous, what my friend Angela calls "done." I think of all the unfixed things in our apartment, the inside of which they've never seen. But they must have studied the floor plan; there must have been ideas, designs they drew on the back of unwanted mail, whispering at their marble counter while they ate dinner side by side. They must have imagined doorways, three bathrooms. The wall between the units coming down, how much they could get done before the baby arrives. Which one would be the child's room. And for the second.

I look at her recessed lighting, the soft throws we each have gathered around our waists—are they cashmere?—and I think, Sure, easy for you to say. Easy the way Lev, for so many years, refused the safety net of his family's money, till now, when someone has to keep up with the mortgage. I haven't done what I wanted either—I thought, like Lev, I'd spend more time in a university—but I wasn't smart enough to pick something else that made money, and whatever I married into was never mine to begin with. Juliet has done both; she, like her husband, works in finance—a smaller firm, she demurred, as if that lessens our difference.

With most of my friends, we drink, but at Juliet's, we eat. She opens bags of pretzels, odd flavors of potato chips she picks up at the deli on her way home. She gives me beautiful cloth napkins on which to wipe my hands. I don't invite her over to our place, nor does she have my number or e-mail. We run into each other in the hallway and we talk too long, and she motions me inside, begs for my company good-naturedly. At Juliet's, I don't have to tell the story I don't yet know how to. It is easier to pretend to relate to her sober; maybe I actually do. She is sweet. She is even, sometimes, funny in a goofy way—unafraid to make herself ugly when telling a story—and she is good at carrying on a conversation about not much at all.

I name the flowers she remembers from the house she grew up in in New Jersey. I can do this by her descriptions alone. "It's insane," she says. "It's a talent."

I wave a blue cheese potato chip in the air with a flourish.

*Busy,* I say to my friends when they ask where I've been. *Overwhelmed.*

I put Lev's name first on the negotiating letters, two more than he permitted me to do. I can do his signature in my sleep. In this way, Juliet and I pretend we are out of it.

"Where will you go?" she asks one night.

"When?"

"After."

"I don't know. Probably to a different neighborhood."

Even if I could afford to stay here, it wouldn't feel right, and though this is close to where I work, I'd rather disappear; I'd rather keep a distance between my failures and a second life that everyone tells me will be so much better.

"Oh, that's too bad," Juliet says. "I'll miss you."

Neither of us mentions the possibility of remaining friends.


Lev and I used to live in different apartments in the same building. We met in the stairwell, under those horrible fluorescent lights, one of us going down, the other headed up. I always took the stairs because there was nothing more interminable than small talk in an elevator; Lev took them to stay in shape, because he sat so much on his couch, laptop warming his legs, that he set a timer to take walking breaks every few hours; some days, if he was on deadline, he'd just climb the eight flights in our building a few times. But one day we talked for so long I began to sweat in my winter coat, my neck slick under my scarf. "I'm keeping you," he kept saying, but I waved him off; I was just running errands, just getting bread. I didn't even need the bread but I was between jobs and had been inside all day and needed to see daylight from outside the apartment. By the time we separated dusk was ending and the streetlights were on. I bought the wrong kind of bread at the corner store, added in a bag of licorice, two oranges from the baskets up front. I needed to feel something weighty that night. I walked with my doubled plastic bags to the park afterward, wanting more air, wanting to not feel so alone from my encounter with Lev, whose name I didn't yet know, who seemed then like the kind of man who was out of my reach, another life I had decided I wouldn't have.

*I like you,* he said the next time he saw me. His honesty was a relief after years dating men who tried to stay one step ahead of me, as if not having mutual feelings was the goal. *Come in,* I said, leading him into my apartment that afternoon. We fell into a routine of being with each other that made sense. We weren't careless.

We quickly dismissed the idea of children; neither of us had the instinct, but we'd never said the choice aloud to anyone else before. The first time we talked about it, we made a verbal list of what we'd gain if we let the idea of it go: money, time with each other. "Think of everything else we'll be able to do," Lev said, relieved. It became a joke to add to the list when we could: sleep, closet space, mugs with curse words on them.

When our upstairs neighbors, Kristen and Ethan, had their two very adorable children, we marked their births by delivering food and offering congratulations, Lev and I giving one another grateful smiles over the bullet we'd dodged. The kids weren't yet in school full-time, and Lev was more than kind about it, all the thumping and the yelping while he worked from his home office, but the vacuuming got to me. So much cleaning. It was exhausting just to listen to.

"I hope they do it every time they vacuum the rug," Lev said one Sunday morning as the overworked machine whirred and hummed above us. He pointed to the ceiling with the blue pencil he used for grading student papers.

Then we heard the sets of feet, the pounding.

"Unlikely," I said, and laughed. Lev cupped my calf under my pants with his free hand. Hours later, after he vacuumed our living room, he insisted on fucking me on the couch in tribute, Kristen and Ethan's family quiet above ours.

When Lev spoke about our hypothetical future—a second house in the Catskills, living abroad for a year or two, even throwing dinner parties (we threw plenty of the other kinds of parties, filled with people and noise; we would crowd the recycling room with our empties, tipping the porters the next morning for the large haul)—it never occurred to me to think about how much he wanted those other things. He was always a talker, and smart enough to see, plainly, how his ambitions didn't match our reality; those fantasies of young adulthood seemed just another party game we played with our friends. I never thought Lev's future wouldn't be linked with mine, that my own contentedness with our present would backfire. *Don't you ever want more?* he asked me in those last few days. I didn't know I was supposed to answer yes.

Here is what we don't talk about at Juliet's: My divorce. Her pregnancy. Our husbands with any specificity beyond "him" or "he." Our other friends, the ones who ask questions we still don't know how to answer. The apartment negotiations, which end with a number Lev tells me is "pushing it," the number I wanted all along.


"That was fast, wasn't it?" Lev says when we meet for a drink the next week to sign the apartment contract, at a bar out of the neighborhood neither of us has been to before. The drink and the neutrality are both Lev's idea. *We did good,* he wrote in a text message, *and we should celebrate.* The bar lighting is low—sad or romantic, depending on your mood.

He has that wild-eyed look about him that tells me he's working, and happy about it. A new book, he lets on as he's inking the date next to his name, in that slow, square handwriting of his that I know he spent hours practicing as a child. "It feels different this time. It's really taking shape." He smiles at me, and without thinking, I smile back, but I don't ask him for details. I put my hands around my drink. I've ordered a bourbon, neat, which is not the way I usually drink, but I want to appear strong to him; I've never thought to before. I wince at a sip of it. Lev has a glass of wine.

I watch him look through the papers in his bag for some document for the building I need to sign, and understand that I don't want to know what he will do with his half of the money, that whatever other life he ends up in will only be a reflection of the one he couldn't have with me, a life I am too afraid to see for fear of wanting it after all. We can't be friends.

Six weeks ago, when he was breaking up with me, he said, "It's better than the alternatives."

I knew he meant cheating, but I wanted to hear him say it. "Which are?" I asked, finally out of shock enough to raise questions.

"Fucking around on each other. Martyrdom. Lies. Take your pick."

Years ago, with friends at the end of a long night of eating and drinking, we debated such a list, created our hierarchies of betrayals: a work girlfriend to flirt with or an alcohol-fueled make-out session in a bar, a stranger or an ex, a series of e-mails or crossing the threshold of a hotel room, a blow job or trading annotated books. I cannot remember which Lev preferred when we had this conversation: the emotional affair or the physical one; years of becoming strangers or the carelessness of a moment. Did I prefer any to divorce?

"It's not about the object," he said that night. "It's about the existing happiness."

"The unhappiness," I jumped in with. We agreed. Our bodies touched under the table.

Should I tell him, now in the bar, after I've signed on the twenty-seven flagged pages, after my whiskey warms my insides to near boiling, about the phone calls from Sam, his friend since college, who had last year decided that I was the better ear than Lev when it came to discussing his own boundaries, which had been in question? "She's destroying me," he said once of his wife, without even saying hello when I answered his call on my lunch break. She had become combative, irresponsible with their money, and though I told him that to start up with some coworker who was showing interest in him was juvenile and wasteful, I did suggest he think long and hard about leaving her, which he did eventually, news to Lev but not to me. Sam, though, takes Lev in the divorce, our divorce.

Sam doesn't call me anymore, and I don't miss it, but fuck him, for making me keep his secrets, and fuck Lev, for insisting in the bar on picking up the bill.

Since Lev left I've started taking the elevator again, those fluorescent lights in the stairways depressing me in a different way. A week after Lev and I sign our papers at the bar, I get into the elevator with Juliet. It's late afternoon, and she isn't in her usual pressed pants and the blouses she has custom-tailored for her "freakishly long arms," as she once described them to me. She has on a pair of sweatpants I've only seen her wear on the couch and a matching sweatshirt; her hair is in a low ponytail. Her diamond earrings are in, though. Traces of makeup—eyeliner, but no lipstick. The in-between of her world face and her home face. She holds her jacket closed with crossed arms. At her door she says, "Come in. Please. James is in Switzerland."

At the end of the kitchen counter where Juliet drops her purse, a neat hook they've installed there, a shelf for keys, a dish for change, there is a package of giant sanitary napkins and a vial of prescription pills with her name on them: Hoffman, same as his. She does not hide them. I do not ask if she is okay. Neither of us is okay. She opens a bottle of wine from a fridge they have just for this, next to their other, larger refrigerator.

"I don't think we can take the apartment anymore," she says as she pours my wine. A drop lands on the countertop; she doesn't wipe it up.

"I understand," I say. "Things change. Things fail."

She splits the plastic sleeve of a roll of crackers down the middle and pushes it toward me.

I tell her what it was like to have Lev say I didn't love him, to offer his forgiveness for a betrayal I hadn't yet considered, for me to watch his face as he watched it register on mine. I never meant to cause him pain. But it's Lev who is always trying to divide things, to draw lines, as if everything and everyone has a boundary, and it's just a question of figuring out where it is and how best to use it.

We get drunk standing in the kitchen, which we litter with cracker crumbs no one moves to sweep into the trash. Juliet opens a second bottle.

The apartment sale is the transaction that will legally, at least, unhook me from Lev forever. The signed contract, clipped behind Juliet and James's deposit check, has been on my coffee table for nearly a week, but I haven't sent it to our lawyer. I promise Juliet I will shred it.

"Will he be mad?" she wants to know.

"Don't worry about it," I say. I did love him. I still do.

Juliet nods her head, her movements so small, but I see them.

I have to pee.

"Mmm-hmm," she says, which is pretty much all she has been getting out as the alcohol gets into her, and as I leave for the bathroom I realize I should stop us, I should stop her. I don't know what those pills are that she's taking, after all.

I've been in this bathroom so many times by now, but never when drunk, and it lends it all a more comfortable familiarity: the Hollywood lights around the mirror, meant to look like something old and glamorous; the penny tile; the matching towels and line of little containers, free of fingerprints. A dear, flawed friend, the life I do not want because I never chose it. I have to trust in my own good sense, years ago. Now.

Before I sit, I notice that the back ridge of Juliet's perfect toilet is rimmed with blood. I think of how one day a tampon hadn't gone down with the first flush and Lev, brushing his teeth, shouted, "Shark!" spitting his toothpaste out in the sink before he did so he could say it as clearly as possible. He stuck his head out the door to make sure I'd heard, so proud of himself, his cleverness, his comfort with his proximity to womanhood.

In Juliet's bathroom, I want to yell it, too, but I won't. My period is a nuisance, but hers, this blood, is that old descriptor: a curse.

I listen for her while I open the medicine cabinet in search of something suitable. They've renovated this space, too, and these hinges don't squeak when I open it, like the ones in our apartment do. It's messy in there: jars of creams stacked sideways, dental floss containers, their jaws open, a puddle of oil; an eyeliner pencil rolls out and falls into the sink. No pill bottles, but what secrets could I want from here anyhow? I use a cotton ball and a dab of body wash from the shower, not worrying about the sucking sound the shower door makes as I open it. Ours rattles, a victim of the misalignment of our floors, which Juliet and James have remedied with demolition, contractors; it will settle, too, with time. When I'm done I wrap the cotton ball in toilet paper, but I know this building's pipes, I worry about it coming back up after I leave. I squish the cotton ball into my pocket, sit down, pee.

Shark.

"Fuck you," I said to Lev that day in the bathroom, and he laughed. I reached past him to flush again. He kissed me on the mouth. Back when he wanted no one else.

# Spider Legs

When I leave to visit my mother in Paris, my father insists on driving me to the airport himself, although I could easily take a cab. The car is buried so deep in the parking garage that we stand at the entrance for twenty minutes before the attendants bring it up. My father speaks to me while staring down the ramp out of which the car is supposed to appear.

"I was thinking, while you're there, you might as well check out the American university."

We've had this conversation before. "I want to go to school in the States," I remind him.

I shift my carry-on bag, heavy with ten days of schoolbooks, from one shoulder to the other. I am missing a week of school for the trip, but it times up with my brother Jack's fall break from college, so I go. My father pushes his hands into his pockets and toes a penny glinting on the garage floor. "Well, perhaps it could be on your list. I hear its art history department is quite good."

"That's Jill, Dad. I like science."

"I know that, Caitlin, but maybe you'll surprise yourself," he snaps at me, but his face is pink with shame.

A car alarm goes off on one of the subbasement floors. We let its bleating take the place of our talking. When it stops, my father says, "I've always thought you might like to spend more time with your mother, that's all," and shakes his head.

"I'm happy here," I say. "I'm happy in New York."

He nods and touches the back of my head affectionately, but he doesn't believe me; I can tell by the furrow still between his eyebrows.

Since their divorce eight years ago, my parents have been shuttling me back and forth between their apartments, and for the past three years, between New York and Paris, where my mother has taken a research fellowship of indeterminate length at the Bibliothèque nationale, ostensibly writing a book. When she left, I moved in with my father and his second-chance family—new wife, new baby. I've never shaken the feeling that he thinks my stay is just temporary.

In the car, my father maintains his strained, guilty silence until he turns on the signal for the airport exit. Then he reminds me, as he likes to periodically, that I don't have to be afraid of Jill and Jack, not on this trip. In this way we share the same deluded hope that this time will be different. He hopes I won't call him in tears asking to come home early, like I did last time, after waiting three hours in a cold spring rain for them to show for a lunch they'd both forgotten about. I can still hear him asking me *why* I had waited so long, a scolding disguised as empathy. But what I hope is that despite seventeen years of feeling like an outsider, on this trip I'll finally find a way in, that I'll stop feeling like an only child.

"I'm not afraid," I say, which is a lie, but I know it's what he wants to hear, though he's not really listening. At the mere thought of them his face has gone hard and defeated, reliving all the anger and suspicion and fear he once had toward them, and the shame that goes along with having those feelings for your own children. He nearly misses my terminal.

At the curb, when I've gathered my bags, his look softens. He pats my shoulder one last time and says, "Be good," as he always does when I leave him, because he knows I will be, because I am not one of his older children, because being good is all I know how to do.

When I see my older brother and sister, John and Jillian—Jack and Jill, as they have always been called—waiting beyond the customs gate at Charles de Gaulle with my mother, my chest tightens. They are like beautiful puzzle pieces, with interlocking features of high cheekbones and broad, easy smiles, the same shade of ashy blond hair tucked behind their ears. My mother still introduces them as Irish twins, no matter how many times Jill reminds her that no one says that anymore. Born less than a year apart, Jack on Jill's heels, they are as close as if they did share a womb, always in each other's friends and lives. Their shared witness of our family's disintegration, the fights I don't recall (including one, they claim, over my being born at all), when they were old enough to understand (or, as my father's new wife says, "know better"), bound them to each other. They always stand behind one another, no matter who stands against them. To me, their fierce loyalty is the inaccessible nucleus of our family.

I expect them to wave and keep walking, as they used to when I was little, shouting to me across the crosswalk that they wouldn't be home for dinner, laughing as they receded, while I headed home. But they don't. Jack takes my bags; my mother pushes my hair out of my face to get a look at me. Jill slings her arm over my shoulder and draws me to her, as if she has been waiting to see me, and while this feels like a mistake—a show, perhaps, for our mother—I let myself sink into her unexpected affection.

In seconds, Jack is under her other arm, laughing at some inside joke of theirs from their mere hours together on French soil. Within a few steps Jill releases me from her grip and I drift back to my mother, who takes my hand and squeezes it. "Here you are," she says to me.

"Here I am," I say.


We go to a late dinner to celebrate my arrival. Jill has been in Paris for a few days already, on vacation from the small, menial jobs she takes and leaves like a series of wrong turns; Jack, since last night. From behind the rim of my glass, I study them as they lean in over their menus. I don't know my brother and sister well, despite these quarterly trips to Paris. While I spent my childhood perfecting how not to be a problem, Jack and Jill were at boarding school, at special summer camps for troubled youth, with tough-love therapists and patient aunts in California. Jill puts down her menu and catches me looking at her; we trade nervous smiles. I fill with the hope that rises up in me at the start of each of these trips: hope that our family can take a form here that we never could in New York, that whatever collective grievances Jill and Jack hold against my parents have faded and won't be used to seal themselves off from the rest of us, that they'll finally see that I can be on their side, too. Maybe it will take longer for us to scatter to different parts of the city as we usually do—Jill and Jack together of course, and I, my mother's sidekick while she pretends that all is fine.

My mother orders champagne; the first glass of it fills my head like a balloon. When it's near-empty, the waiter asks if we want another bottle. Jill says yes. "We might as well, right?" She winks right at me.

When we're done with the meal, Jack takes out a cigarette. He tips the pack toward Jill.

"Don't anymore."

"Really?"

"Five months," she says.

"That's great," Mom says, reaching over to pat Jill's hand approvingly. "Now's the time to quit, while you're young." Her eyes are glassy from the champagne.

"By week's end, you'll be back," Jack says before sliding the pack into his coat pocket, his mouth crumpled into childish displeasure.

Mom turns to me, asks, "How's your dad doing?" My father

will ask about her when I return, these public displays of civility part of the play they've put on for me since the split.

"Oh, yes, how is Father?" Jill's voice is heavy with sarcasm. Jill lives in New York, too, but we don't see her much; she and my father like it that way.

"He's fine. You know. He drove me to the airport."

"Did he bring the worm with him?" Jill crosses her eyes and wiggles her finger up and down, making Jack snicker.

"The worm" is their nickname for our half sister, Hope; she's four now. My father brings her along when he doesn't know what to say to us.

"No, just us."

"Lucky you," Jack says. Jill laughs, snorting a bit as she takes a sip of water.

My mother is too busy counting out bills from her wallet for the check, her eyes squinting in concentration, to say anything.

The four of us walk home that night along the Seine, waving giddily at the Bateaux Mouches, the big tourist boats, as they pass.

The next day, my mother meets me in the Luxembourg Gardens for lunch. I bring us sandwiches from her favorite boulangerie, near the apartment. We sit on green metal chairs, watching the birds in the fountains, watching people.

"You know, I was thinking maybe you'd want to come here for the summer," she says as she unwraps the paper from her sandwich. She tried to get me to stay with her last summer.

"Maybe." I don't want to make another trip; I want her to come home. The longer my mother works here, the older she looks, the stranger she dresses, and, I think, the happier she becomes.

"How is the book?" I ask her. She seems busier than she was during our last visit—more time at the library, longer hours.

"Good, really good," she says as she hands me a napkin, catching a tomato sliding out from my baguette. "The research part of it's almost done. Now comes the writing."

"You can do that at home, can't you? In New York?"

My mother puts her sandwich in her lap and takes my hand between hers. "Caitlin, look, I'm selling the New York apartment."

I spent my childhood in that apartment; we stayed in it after the divorce. A couple is renting it now with all the furniture, and when I walk by there on my way to flute lessons I think of them and their two young children, living a life we never had in its walls—quiet, harmonious, intact. I probably won't see the apartment again, won't absentmindedly smooth the paper that's peeling back toward the walls, won't get a salute from Boris, the weekend doorman, or wait for the telltale flicker of the elevator lights before our floor.

"Why?" I ask.

"Paris is my home now."

"But it's not mine."

"It could be, if you'd let it."

I look at my mother in this park in Paris where walking across the grass is a crime, at her soft, proud face, and I think, What could she know about home, about families, this woman who moved thousands of miles away from her own? I shake my head. "Don't you care about where I want to be?"

"Of course I care."

"It doesn't feel that way."

I pull my hand from hers, return to my sandwich. It's a beautiful late-fall day, and the park is full of people having lunch, reading *Le Monde*, of tourists snapping photos under the foliage at the Medici Fountain. The voices of foreigners are all around me, speaking French and German and Japanese and Czech. My mother's voice, as she tries to explain why the move is good for all of us, is the only one I can understand. I let it bleed into the others, let it become foreign.

I don't expect to see Jack and Jill at the apartment, but they're there, finishing their own sandwiches at the small counter that divides the kitchen from the rest of the living space.

"What happened to you?" Jack asks.

"She's selling the apartment, in New York," I say, taking off my coat.

"That's too bad," he says, crumpling up the paper from his sandwich and aiming it at the trash can.

"Thank God," Jill says. "That place is cursed."

"Jill." Jack thwacks her on her shoulder with his knuckles, indicates me with his head.

"It's okay," I say, too quickly, because I don't want them to feel sorry for me.

"Oh, come on," Jill says to Jack. "The worst years of our childhood happened after we moved into that apartment." We moved a year after I was born. "I think Caitlin can handle that not all of us have fond memories of it."

"Sure I can," I say, and pull my calculus textbook from my

backpack in the living room. I take a seat at the end of the counter.

Jack peers over my shoulder. "You're sad and you're doing math?" He shakes his head.

Jill reaches over him and closes my textbook. "No, no homework today. We need to do something fun. We need an adventure."

I've been trained by my parents to think that my difference in disposition from Jill and Jack is best for me—that I'm too young, too good to get mixed up in the trouble they always seem to get into, but all I've ever wanted is to go where they go without me.

That afternoon, Jack and I follow Jill from shop to shop, letting her dress us like dolls. She wraps Jack in scarves until she finds one she deems acceptable, a stretch of steel gray cashmere she carefully coils around his neck. "So handsome," she gushes, and she means it. Jack nods in appreciation.

For me, Jill chooses shoes from a small shop in the Marais. They are a warm pink suede, slim and sophisticated, with a tiny heel. When I look at myself in the store mirror, my jeans pulled up to reveal ankles marked by sock elastic, it seems the top and bottom parts of myself are two different people: the ponytailed, lightly freckled face of a child, and the calves of a woman now shaped by the small lift of that heel. Jill smiles at me in the mirror.

"They're beautiful," she says.

"They're more you. You should try them on."

"No, they're yours. We'll get them."

I stand in bare feet as she puts them back in the box, tucking the tissue paper over them. She pays for them with Mom's credit card.

At my mother's request, I stop at the library before dinner the next night. It's empty of its tourists and most of the other scholars, of the people who have people to go home to at night. Before we go into her private reading room, we wash our hands in the small bathroom down the hall. There's only one sink, and we let our hands run under the tap at the same time, the way we used to when I was a child.

In the study room, the walls are stenciled in French with the rules for handling the materials, the *ne*s stacking up neatly, a tower of don'ts. There's a laptop, its screen dark, on a pile of books on one desk. "Come here; I want to show you something," my mother says, her voice soft and secretive, as though I'm still a girl. On a large table at the other end of the room, an open manuscript waits, fragile and faded and beautiful. We slide on pairs of cotton gloves, and she nods me toward it.

Saint Agnes, she explains, one of the patron saints of girls, the subject of her book. Agnes, beautiful and rich, was a prize, even at twelve. But she chose God over men, religion over marriage. She feared no punishment; she refused the offers of marriage that would have saved her from public humiliation, her eventual beheading. When given one last chance, brought into the temple to worship the goddess the Romans then revered, she crossed herself instead.

"For that, she was tortured, shamed, killed, of course." My mother clicks her tongue. "No sense of self-preservation, those saints," she says, and smiles.

There's a sword at Agnes's throat, but Agnes, pious, haloed, looks calm, accepting; this manuscript is one of only a handful to depict her like this. It's rare, my mother says, to see such an image of her. "Mostly, they like to show her with lambs."

"It's nice," I say after a pause, unsure what she wants me to say.

"It's special, and I wanted you to see it. Just you."

She gives me this look I recognize from the divorce, the one that asks for my silent understanding, to be on her side. I was only seven then, when the family really started to fall apart. I can still see her so clearly by the phone in the hall, a hand covering her forehead, asking, "*Where?*" already reaching for her coat and keys on their hooks. And then she'd give me that weak smile that asked me not to have seen anything at all, because by then she'd stopped telling my father about those phone calls, about the places she'd go to pick up Jill and Jack: police stations, store security offices, and once, when he was away on a business trip, the outermost tip of Long Island; she'd had to rent a car to bring them back that time. "He isn't built for children," she said to me one night, sitting on the edge of my bed. I'd woken up because my father had found out about one such omission and pounded a fist against the dining room wall, which was also the wall to my bedroom. "Your brother and sister, they're just *too much* for him." The rings under her eyes suggested they were too much for her, but she never said so. She tucked the covers in firmly, as if to hold me in place.

She shuts off the light above the manuscript. "I think I'm going to skip dinner tonight; I'm not too hungry anyway. But you guys go, and have a good time." My mother loves the library at night, its promised emptiness. She's made friends with the night guards, who check on her before they go off shift. "You know how it is; I just get so caught up in it." She gestures to the room around her. She forgets I am only seventeen, that I do not know how anything is.

She reaches for her purse and pulls out some cash. "Take a cab to dinner, won't you?"

I take the money from her, but I walk. My new shoes, which she did not notice, still feel good on my feet, and it's only a few blocks to the restaurant.

At dinner, Jack and Jill's way of looking out for the hurt that must be on my face is to keep ordering wine. *Un de plus, un de plus,* they say, touching the tip of the empty carafe each time.

Jill holds the lip of a fresh carafe over my glass, which is still half-full. "You want more?" she asks, but this is not really a question. It's a test, a dare, an invitation.

"Sure," I say.

"'Atta girl," Jack says, and they both beam their smiles onto me.

After a few glasses of wine, Jack begins to tell stories from their adolescence, of the years during the divorce, of the places they'd run off to—the park, mostly, and friends' houses, and candy stores on the East Side, where they'd have competitions to see who could pocket the most candy.

"It wasn't as much fun as he makes it sound," Jill says as she exhales smoke from the side of her mouth—her first cigarette in five months. "I mean, we also used to pretend we were orphans."

"It was fun, and you know it," Jack says, and tips the pack of cigarettes to me. Jill swats it away. "Dad would kill you," she says to both of us, and I leave the cigarettes alone.

We stay out drinking till the waiters start lifting chairs onto the tables to sweep underneath. We walk out into the crisp night of fall drunk, full, pleased with ourselves. We decide to head to the Louvre to see the pyramid all lit up. Jack has the remainders of a bottle of wine he swiped from a table before the waiters got to it tucked into his peacoat.

They whisper the plan to me, my brother in one ear, my sister in the other, as if they are speaking to one another through me. "So when the cab stops, you run," Jill says, smoothing my hair back behind my ear. "We'll come find you," Jack assures me as he hails a cab over to us. They shut the door before I can protest. I'm too drunk to say otherwise.

I can see the cabby's jowls shake as he looks for the corner Jill has told him to stop at, a false address she delivered in her best French, with a smile.

When the moment comes, Jack tries to pull me in his direction by my jacket, but I freeze. I run away from the cab, back in the direction we've come from, to look for a bridge the cab can't cross, or a dark place to hide and wait for my siblings to come find me.

The cab sits in the middle of the block, its back doors open. For a few moments, the only sounds in the empty street are our footsteps pounding off in three directions. And then below the thrum of my heartbeat, I hear doors slamming, and tires squealing, and then the car is behind me, closing in.

I can't get out of the streetlights; there is no bridge. I try to turn a corner, but the heel of my beautiful new shoe gives out under me, and my ankle takes a sharp twist; I fall forward into the curb.

I give up. The knee of one pant leg has split. My chest heaves wildly with my sobs. The cab's headlights illuminate the street that I planned to escape to, a quiet residential block. When the driver gets out, he curses me in French. Shaking, I offer him the francs I have in my pocket, the remainder of the money my mother gave me. "C'est tout," I manage, *all I have.* He bends down, the folds of his fat face gathered up in disgust, grabs my elbow on the arm that holds the francs, and shoves me backward. The coins spill into the street. He raises an arm; he is going to strike me. I cover my face, bracing myself.

Instead he spits on me, spreading an ounce of thick phlegm that smells like tobacco over my fingertips and hair. "Salope!" he shouts at me before he gets in his cab and drives away. I don't know what this means, but I can tell from the way he says it that it is something awful.

When Jill and Jack arrive, their faces are flushed and healthy. "There you are," Jack says, as if I have pulled off a very good game of hide and seek.

"What happened?" Jill asks, confused.

I shake my head. I don't want to cry in front of them, but I can't help it. My lungs feel as scraped as the heels of my hands, and I cough before I am able to speak. "He chased me."

Jack looks around, sees the skid marks on the street. "With the car?" he asks.

I nod at their knees; they both stand back from me in the empty street.

"You're okay." Jill bends over to put a hand on my shoulder. "You're fine," she says to me, sugar in her voice. I push her hand off.

Jack's fingertips encircle my elbow and try to lift me. "Why don't we walk a little?"

I don't answer. I make myself heavy on the sidewalk. Jack looks back at Jill from his crouched position in front of me; I hear her long exhale.

"We're just a few blocks from the pyramid. We'll sit; we'll have a drink," Jill says, rubbing her arms in the cold.

"I can't," I say.

"Sure you can. You'll feel better when we get there."

The shoes dig into my flesh as my foot continues to swell. I am trying not to feel it, but I know blood is pooling in between my toes. I'm filled with a sudden hatred for the shoes; I take them off and put them on the sidewalk beside me.

"Shit," Jill says as she notices my bloody pinky toe. Most of the nail has come off.

Jack sits down on the curb next to me. He puts both arms around me, and pulls me in close. I've never been here before, so buried in his chest, but I imagine that Jill has, after a breakup or a failed test or during the divorce. My brother squeezes me with a force meant to bring me back to strength, but the weight of my own foolishness overwhelms me; I hate that I have done exactly as I've been told. And while I want most to shove him away, I don't.

"We can't stay here," Jill says to Jack, her voice antsy now.

"Give her a minute," he says.

I'm still crying into his jacket, the wine bottle in his inside pocket pushing against my ribs, but I sense them mouthing to each other over me, hear Jill's impatient pacing behind me. I feel his arm lift and she stops. A flash of jealousy stirs in my stomach, knowing they are speaking without even needing words.

When we were growing up, our mother showed us everything that was magical to children: the mechanical bear that blew bubbles outside the Penny Whistle toy shop, the quiet beauty of night-sledding in Central Park, how to lengthen our shadows in the streetlights across the sidewalks of Manhattan. Mom, Jill, Jack, and I would walk the dogs we'd picked out at the pound after the divorce on Central Park West, and I'd stretch my arms up so far I'd lose sight of my hands in the distance, and give myself long spider legs, thick and lengthy and strong as they weren't yet. But then Jack would run up behind me and eclipse my shadow with his, and Jill would climb onto his back from a park bench to make it even larger. They became a giant bug with six legs and massive wings; they pretended to devour me. My mother laughed; we all laughed then.

Jill finally sits on the other side of me. She takes off her shoes, uses the hem of her shirt to wipe mine out, and puts them on her own feet, broken heel and all. "Here," she says, sliding hers toward me. They are half a size too big, but I put them on. "Let's go," she says a final time.

Before bed, I notice my broken, bloodied shoes in the closet. I throw them into the trash, taking satisfaction in their thud against the metal bucket, and go to sleep. When my mother asks about the scrapes on my hands at dinner the next night, I tell her I tripped in my new shoes coming out of the Metro, and neither Jack nor Jill says a word.

I am scheduled to leave Paris on a Sunday night. Jack has already gone back to Boston; he muttered an apology as he hugged me good-bye, and while it felt like he meant it, I couldn't look him in the eye as we separated. I decide to take a walk in the morning, the apartment feeling too full of people still. My mother is sleeping in; the library is shut all day, even to her. Jill is packing in her room when I put my coat on. She sticks her head out the door, asks me where I'm going.

"Just a walk."

"You want company?"

"Not really," I say. Maybe what I see on her face is hurt, or a kind of apology; I'm not sure she'd ever let either show.

"I might not be here. My train leaves at noon. Will you be back?" Jill is heading to London to see friends. She hasn't said so, but I suspect there isn't much waiting for her in New York except me and Dad.

"Probably not."

"I'll see you when I get back, then?" She puts her arms out for a hug.

"Sure," I say into her ear as she squeezes me, but I don't expect her to call.

It's not ten yet, but near Notre Dame there is a crowd gathering for Mass. I weave through the swell of the devout the way I learned to as a child of New York, trusting that there is an open space just beyond the bodies moving against the direction I want to go in. When I get there, to a small street on the Île de la Cité, I hear the bells calling people in to services.

I keep going till the streets get quieter and emptier. When I find a small cathedral at the end of a narrow street, its simple gray facade is a relief to me, and I pull open the door without asking myself why. I'm wearing my American sneakers; they're silent in a sea of Sunday shoes clicking on the stone floor. It's cold in the church, and I can see my breath in the light coming through the stained-glass windows. The service hasn't begun yet, but the church is full of people settling into their pews, pulling their coats tight around them in the chill morning air.

I stand off to the side in the nave and look for the saints I know—the ones my mother has taught me—in the stained glass, but they are not there: not Lucy, not Agnes with her lambs, not even Genevieve, the patron saint of Paris. What my mother says has always fascinated her about the saints is the basic question of their existence, how little proof the faithful needed. Some saints didn't really exist, except through art and images and stories, through the collective imaginings of those who wanted to believe in them.

The things I want I can't will into existence: a version of my family that never was, a place we can all agree on as home. And maybe I am like my father, not built for this, not built for siblings, or family, or Jack and Jill. Perhaps it's a gene, a predisposition. When I think of it this way, as a malfunction, it doesn't hurt so much, though it seems like a waste of time, all these years of me trying to fit into them when I cannot, not by my nature, not by theirs. I understand what my parents have known for years: I am the proof, the last to verify that this thing we tried to make a family doesn't work; I am the piece that belongs in a different box, that comes from a different puzzle altogether.

As the service begins, a young woman slides over to make room for me in her pew. I hadn't planned to stay, but I nod my head in gratitude. And even though I don't believe, I take a seat.

# Weighed and Measured

*Birdsong*

The summer she is fourteen, Franny doesn't want to do much at all. Everyone else she knows is away at summer camp, but she has never much liked camp. She can't sleep with all those other girls close by, breathing and turning in the dark, the sounds of their sheets, of their jaws moving in dreams. She doesn't like bugs or the outdoors or dividing into teams. She likes the empty heat of the city, the bad luck of an un-air-conditioned subway car, the routine she and Lucia fall into by the second week of July: making plans they abandon by mid-morning on account of a thunderstorm or the humidity or money, instead often wandering from Lucia's parents' apartment in Hell's Kitchen, where Franny is permitted to sleep over two nights a week, toward the park for some shade. Both girls are only children whose parents work full-time. Good girls. Of course Franny's parents say yes to her spending the summer this way.

If they are hungry, they stop at the pizza place on Ninth Avenue, taking seats as far from the oven as they can. They get cold sodas on their way out the door. Lucia pops hers immediately, but Franny waits till they are in the park. Today, she leans against a tree trunk and puts the cold can between her fairly recent breasts inside her shirt. "Gross," says Lucia. "You know where that's been? There's rat shit on those cans." She will only drink out of a straw. Lucia's breasts couldn't hold up a penny, but when she talks about them to Franny she calls them tits. Lucia likes to make her laugh.

"There's rat shit everywhere in this city," says Franny. "What do you think you're sitting on now?"

"Uh, duh, the grass."

"Trust me, a rat has shit there, too."

"I can't wait to get out of here," Lucia says, sucking the last of her Sprite up through the straw.

Franny shrugs. She listens to Lucia talk about the other places she wants to be, the not-here, a vague soliloquy about air and quiet. The grass that won't have rat shit or dog pee or beer caps or empty dime bags on it. It will not have anyone you don't know or want within inches—feet, yards, miles, if you are lucky—on it either.

"Birds," says Lucia.

"What's so great about birds?" Franny asks. "They have no arms. They freak me out."

"They sing."

"They sing here, too," she says. "Listen. Close your eyes."

Lucia makes a face but does it and they hear them, they do,

but also sirens and some kid having a tantrum in a playground Franny thought was farther away. The loop of the ice-cream truck's song, which Franny's mother says will drive her to homicide. Whistles and thwaps and everything in contact with something else.

"I only want the birdsong," Lucia says when she opens her eyes.

Franny is about to say that where Lucia wants to go sounds a lot like camp, but then she remembers Lucia saying her parents wouldn't ever spend the money on that sort of thing. She said Franny was crazy not to go.

*Why would you stay here?*

*Camp's not that great.*

The girls were always nice to Franny, but it's not the same as it is with Lucia, who she can say anything to, who she can sleep next to peacefully.

*Sounds great.*

*Next summer, you pretend to be me.*

*Next year, we'll go together.*

How easily Lucia would fit in there, how good she is at assuming she belongs everywhere.

They go back to Lucia's apartment and take turns in a cold shower, after which they try on each other's clothes in pursuit of what feels the lightest against their skin. Lucia borrows a dress of Franny's that's short on her, but she is all legs, and doesn't mind that they are exposed, that if she steps over a sidewalk grate at the wrong time, the dress might lift up. The bust is loose where it hugs Franny tightly, enough so that she thinks she should just give it to Lucia, and she does, but Lucia returns it when the summer is over, and neither one wears it ever again. On that day in her room, Lucia tugs the hem down in front of the mirror, and turns back to Franny. Then she fans herself between her legs. "This is what I need. Air up in here." Franny snorts.

Franny wears the same denim shorts she wore earlier—she laid them on top of the air conditioner while she showered, and they are deliciously cold against her thighs, for now. She borrows a T-shirt of Lucia's that is soft and light and large—too big, Lucia says; she only sleeps in it, but Franny likes how it hangs, not so big that she is lost in it, but safe. Later that night, as they are walking down Seventh Avenue, Lucia will say it is her cousin Patrick's, and that Franny will like him. He is coming in August, from upstate, staying with them for a few weeks while his mother moves back to the Bronx. The girls walk all the way to the East Village, hunting a coolness that they give up on, that anyone who is left in the city in summer gives up on. Lucia's hair curls at her brow, but she doesn't—on this night, at least—complain. Almost back at the apartment, Franny's heel blistered from wearing sneakers without socks, men make noises at them like the old women make to get the pigeons closer. One of the men calls out to them in Spanish. Lucia's face goes hot.

"What did he say?" Franny asks as they step under the awning of Lucia's building.

Her friend shakes her head.

The air conditioner in Lucia's room is out, so they sleep with a window propped open, one fan whirring. Franny listens for the birdsong, but Lucia is right; the city is all traffic and music from speakers, all the human noises that scare the birds.

## Are You Experienced?

Lucia joins the cross-country team that fall; early on Saturday mornings, Franny goes with the cousin, Patrick, to the meets. Before the race starts, the team stretches. In between stretches they clap hands, but their timing is never perfect, so it's like an echo, a chain of noise in between their murmuring, in between bends and rolls and hands on each other's shoulders as they hold their ankles to their waists. Hamstrings, quads, hips, shins. Franny watches Lucia shake her legs out on the starting line, her friend looking like someone else, like a girl who wants something she can see in the distance, hungry, maybe; mean, like she isn't in real life. And then, in a moment, catching Franny's eye, smiling, and again she is like who Franny knows she is.

They watch Lucia run into the woods, and wait for her to come out of them, twenty-three minutes of the cross-country course where she can't be seen. Franny and Patrick walk the outer edge of the park together while Lucia's parents wait at the finish line, drinking coffee with the others.

One Saturday, Lucia takes fifth in the meet, making her the fastest on the school's team, and she's only a freshman. After, in the backyard of a house in Yonkers that belongs to Patrick's mother's boyfriend, Lucia untangles Franny's necklace for her, a silver chain with a single cursive *F* charm, without even looking at her long, thin fingers at work. Patrick and Franny are talking about camping, about stars, about wild animals. Lucia lowers the necklace onto the lap of her skirt between her thumbs and pointers, the chain a single knot from done. "Where I come from—" she starts to say, but Patrick cuts her off: "You were born at Montefiore; you come from the Bronx."

It's then that Franny, on her way to the bathroom inside, steps on a bee. "Fuck," she says, over and over, each one a little softer, till it's just a whisper. Patrick stomps on the already-dead bee with his sneaker. Lucia gets ice from the house, which she holds against Franny's swollen heel while Patrick stands over them, hands on his hips, looking for something to do. He catches Franny's eye. "Who needs wild animals?" he says, the small space between his incisors showing in his smile. Franny holds her own ice and Lucia finishes the necklace and puts it on for her, lifting Franny's hair and letting it down again.

"Gracias," Franny says.

"De nada, chica."

There is dinner, inside, because of the bees—even though Lucia prefers, always, to be outside, the mothers have decided, and there are no arguments about it. The way the women are together is its own foreign country; they move around each other like extensions of a single body, their voices and laughter entangled. For a few years, the sisters weren't speaking, but that's behind them now, a story Lucia promises she'll tell Franny but never gets around to. All summer Franny and Lucia claimed to be sisters, cousins sometimes, though who would believe it: Franny blond and green-eyed and compact, edgeless; Lucia, long limbed and straight-faced, her hair black and wavy. Around

Lucia's and Patrick's mothers Franny understands that what's between her and Lucia can always be broken, that it will.

On the weekends when Patrick doesn't come to the city, they visit him at boarding school, where he is on scholarship. Patrick is Puerto Rican, like Lucia, but no one at school believes him, because he is tall and lean and freckled, like any other prep school boy, his hair almost red in the fall sunlight. Plus, his name. *My father's Irish,* he'd explain, and maybe he is, but no one except his mother knows that for certain, and she won't tell him anything he wants to know. *For what,* she asks, *would it do you any good?*

One visit, before Patrick's and Lucia's mothers take them out to dinner—a tacky Polynesian place two towns over they all love, with its dry-ice volcanoes and plastic mermaids in the drinks—Patrick takes off his shirt in front of the girls, his long, pale torso something Franny wants to turn away from but doesn't.

She sits on his lap one Sunday afternoon in his dorm room while Lucia is out in the woods, smoking with Patrick's roommate, and he says, "It's okay," because he can feel her hovering, worried about letting her weight onto him. He pretends it doesn't matter, and so she does, too. Her heart thumps. He hums a song she doesn't know. The smoking spot is a good fifteen minutes from the dorm, but it's taken ten minutes to just make it to this point, and how much time do they have? He touches her back through her shirt, a warm hand on the nubs of her spine. He is moving slow; he is waiting. But she's never asked him to. She will have him wait forever. She will never kiss him. She feels him hard under her leg, and she wishes she didn't, that she had never agreed to be gathered into his arms on this futon, but the power. The power of her vibrates.

The next weekend, Patrick visits the city, which has been sieged by rain. He throws Franny, at her request, over and over, onto Lucia's bed. Her body compared to his is small, collapsible. One time, her ankles hit the wall. She cries out in pain, in laughter. Lucia gives them looks from a chair across the room. No, she doesn't want a turn. She says she has a headache, puts her hand over her eyes. Patrick and Franny go outside under a single umbrella and buy her junk at the drugstore: a pair of neon green slippers, a pack of watermelon-flavored gum, a magazine for girls who love horses that they laugh so hard at in the store that Franny's muscles are sore the next day. When they get back to the apartment, Franny crawls into bed beside Lucia with the bag, which, wet from the rain, drips water onto the blanket.

It is nearly midnight in June when, over the phone, Patrick tells Franny he's in love with her, and her silence is so long and so deep she falls into a quick sort of dream, a half-conscious flash of her backyard in winter. He is done with school; she still has three more weeks of ninth grade. He is two years older but only a grade ahead; this was the only way the school would take him, on repeat. Her dream is broken by his asking, "You still there?"

How is she supposed to respond? She loves riding in the car he drives (his mother's), the windows down, silent except for a tape he's made for her, though he doesn't say this exactly, doesn't say it's for her, but he knows it and she knows it so she listens extra hard. They don't tell Lucia about that weekend, during Patrick's spring break, March. Lucia was away, visiting her grandmother, the one she and Patrick don't share. Patrick parked at the end of a hiking trail they'd not worn the right shoes to walk, their car the only one there. He suggested they smoke a joint, but Franny, suddenly worried, said no. "It's okay," he said, "not a big deal," and opened the sunroof, and popped their seats back, wiggling his eyebrows at her above his sunglasses. When, after a few minutes of watching the clouds, he asked her what she was so afraid of, it was a genuine question. She tried to answer, but the best she could do was to say, "I don't know." She considered laying her head on his chest. She saw that he wanted to rip her open, and she was afraid of his body, of what it might mean to allow him to show her everything she did not yet know.

On the phone she says, "I'm here," and he waits, as he often does, for a more complete answer.

## Wish You Were Here

They heard that cows like to be sung to, so one night during that week at the rental house in Vermont, on their way back from the dairy barn, they take their ice cream to the fence and fight over which song to sing.

Lucia wants to sing "Happy Birthday," but Patrick refuses, so then she suggests a song in Spanish—one that Franny won't know—and Patrick shoots that down, too.

"I got it," he says, and makes the last of his cone disappear in one bite, then hooks his arms over the fence. They are scratched from where he climbed into some raspberry bushes earlier that morning, his arms marked by a combination of dots and dashes, freckles and the light scrapes from the thorns. The cows are far out in the field, clustered together.

*So . . . so you think you can tell . . .* Patrick's voice is shaky, deeper than Franny has ever noticed it when he sings along in the car. At the end of the summer he will be a junior at school; he will date a girl from Connecticut, with shiny dark hair and her own credit cards, who Franny will never meet.

"What song is this?" Lucia asks.

"Pink Floyd," Franny says, and joins Patrick at the fence. She starts singing, too.

Lucia holds her ice-cream cone but doesn't eat it. "I don't know this song."

*We're just two lost souls swimming in a fishbowl . . .*

The cows haven't even turned an eye. Their tails swat away the flies. Patrick's and Franny's voices barely fill the space between them.

Lucia throws her cone over the fence. She wipes her hands with the small white napkin she still holds. "They're not coming. They don't care," she says before she starts walking toward the house, dropping the napkin to the ground. Franny and Patrick stay; they finish the song. Franny picks up Lucia's trash, crumpling it in the palm of her hand.

"I got this," Patrick says to Franny, before he catches up to Lucia, who he challenges to a race. Franny watches them run ahead, anticipates the moment when Lucia extends an arm to shove her cousin aside, even though she could beat him without it. "Cheater!" Patrick yells as he tries to push her back, but she's out of his reach already. "Asshole!" Lucia yells back, three leg lengths ahead of him.

The three of them fall asleep in one room, on the two twin beds the girls have pushed together underneath the window, Lucia in the middle, her hair over her face. The lights are already out when Patrick reaches one of his long arms over to tap Franny on the crown of her head. Franny lifts her head, mouths *hello*. They snort with laughter. The bed shakes, but Lucia doesn't wake up, not for the next hour while they talk over her sleeping body.

The next morning, Franny wakes to the cousins fighting in the living room, yelling that Franny can't untangle the meaning of. Neither one looks at her as she enters the room. Patrick's mother is in the kitchen cracking eggs into a metal bowl, a pile of eggshells on the counter next to it. Patrick's nostrils flare in annoyance as Lucia leans into him, her bare arms crossed at her chest. "It's not your choice," Lucia says. Lucia's mother snaps at them in Spanish and they stop.

"He doesn't understand," Lucia says, in English.

"Oh, I understand," Patrick says.

He stares Lucia down till she goes outside. He looks right past Franny as she follows her out, carrying a sweatshirt that she drops onto Lucia's head by its hood. She doesn't ask her why she is crying, or what they were fighting about. She hooks her arm through Lucia's and they start walking out into the field behind the house, though they are both still in pajamas. The grass is wet with dew; Franny wishes she had shoes on.

Lucia stops walking to put her arms through the sleeves of the sweatshirt.

"He can't get everything good; he can't have it all to himself."

"Of course not," Franny says, but she doesn't know what Lucia is talking about; her friend has to work her way backward to it, to the fact that she, too, has just been offered a spot at Patrick's school.

"It's not like I won't have my own life," Lucia says.

"You will," Franny says, and tries not to cry herself.

## Dog Walks

Sixteen was the last year to be weighed and measured, to bend over and touch her toes in the pale pink exam room of the pediatrician, birds of the world poster at the level of her nose, her waist. Her spine examined, her knees tapped. Franny's mother sat with a book in the waiting room, only there to pay the bill, to get her daughter back to school afterward. An adult doctor would do soon; a gynecologist was in order, too. Her growing more or less done. *Beautiful,* the doctor said in her office afterward, scanning all of Franny's numbers over the rim of hot pink reading glasses, as she had since Franny's parents first brought her in, at the start of the charting, the perfectly rising curve. *So smart,* the doctor said during those early visits, after hearing Franny speak and, later, read and interrupt her parents to give answers she thought she had. *How many words? Fifty? A hundred?*

Franny remembers when the body was beautiful just because it worked. Three and four and six and nine. She remembers where she could fit. On her father's shoulders; on the dog, the little one, dead for over five years now, straining on the leash in front of them as they walked around their block weekend afternoons; on her mother's lap, their legs a jumble. Each place outgrown.

When a boy about her size unzips her pants and his own late one night at his apartment, yanking her underwear at the bumps of her hips, Franny says no, asks what he's doing. It's ten o'clock on a late summer night, and the boy's parents are out of town for the weekend. Another only child. As she gets up from this boy's bed, her back hot from being pressed against his comforter, she feels stupid for having wanted to be here in the first place. She doesn't know what she was after.

Earlier that day, Lucia left for boarding school. That first year away, she will fall in and out of love with two different boys. She will try to explain it to Franny in letters, and for a few months over the phone, but Franny will understand Lucia less and less; she will find it hard to remember what she is like, what they were like. On her end of the telephone, Franny will feel the pressing of the secrets she's keeping from her, including, now, this one: how the boy made her think of Patrick, the game they played, him lifting her up and dropping her down onto the bed, her sudden understanding of how a girl can have something taken from her.

She loses Lucia's number, Patrick's, too. Loosens them from her mind the way she loosened herself from Patrick's lap that afternoon in his dorm, sliding back to a more innocent place so that when Lucia came in, her cheeks pink with the cold of the Connecticut woods, she didn't even ask what they had done while she was gone, why Patrick was in a mood, looking out the window. The rest of that weekend, Lucia was on Patrick's case for being so serious, for not introducing them to any of the boys down the hall like he had said he would.

## Sweetheart

She's eighteen the first time she has sex, with a boy named Eric. She's twenty-two by the time she thinks she loves someone. His name is Will. She tells herself she can love him without wanting anything from him. She knows if she wants something—her lips against his bare biceps, his feet hanging off the edge of the twin bed she still slept in in that first apartment (Washington Heights; three roommates)—she will want everything. A cascade.

There are the years when she thinks the only answers are the body. The spring she is twenty-five, it is Benji's body she thinks about the most, but they've never touched. In the school where they work he walks by her desk five or six times a day, sometimes with his class of third-graders, sometimes on his way to the faculty lounge, which she knows is quicker reached by a different route. When no one else is there to see, he taps his fingers on her desktop in greeting.

In the corners of rooms where he talks to her, in the hours they spend in a bar, before his live-in girlfriend finishes her workday, Franny calls him sweetheart. She wants him to imagine, just for a moment, that she owns him. She wants to plant that possibility in his mind, even if he dumps it out immediately. "Yes, honey," he says back, sarcastically, but he does not mean it. She doesn't touch him, but for the hours afterward she imagines she did, then his fingers on her, inside her. "Fuck," she says aloud in the elevator of her apartment building, when she is finally alone. She imagines the relief of not wanting him anymore, the end of the pain of wanting pleasure.

In this, she can't help but think of Patrick, how long he bore what she now knows is unbearable. Sweetheart. She never could command her body to want his; the way she loved him would never have been enough. She could control her desire for him just as much as she could the tears Lucia wanted when their friendship was ending, that she went so far as to ask for, in a letter Franny kept for a month and then just threw away, never writing back. *How come you never cried when we fought? Did you just not care?* Franny now is a rare crier, and does so silently, so if she ever had, on the other end of a call with Lucia or Patrick, they might never have known it was happening at all.

# American Men in Paris
# I Did Not Love

Andrew, who finds me reading on the floor of the American Library, in the corner where two stacks meet. At my feet, near the toes of the boots I have spent too much money on, four or five books, of no real interest to me beyond the fact that their pages are filled with English words, and I am already tired of French—of collecting new words, of the steps it takes to understand it, of how, when I choose not to, there isn't a silence but a loneliness, the low hum of a life that never will be second nature to me.

Andrew, older, both in years and in worldliness. The American university we attend is his third school in five years, punctuated by travel, by an indecisiveness I, not knowing any better, admire, covet, even. Andrew picks up the books, passing them from one hand to the other, feigning his interest in the pages. He taps a closed one against my knee gently, says we should get a drink sometime. And when we do, at a bar in an arrondissement farther out than I've yet been brave enough to venture, we talk about the lit class we are in together, where I am the youngest, two months into eighteen.

"How did you get in?" he wants to know on the Metro on the way over.

The professor read my admissions essays; she asked to have me in the class, usually reserved for juniors and seniors, none of whom are particularly nice to me. Andrew purses his lips, nods his head, impressed. I believed then that a man might be interested in me only for my intelligence.

He tells me the bar we're at once sold coal across its zinc bar top. We sit at a table in the center of the room and order a bottle of wine; Andrew says something about how he'll take care of whatever I don't want to drink. We finish two bottles. He orders oysters but I don't eat any.

"My throat closes," I explain.

"Allergic?" he asks.

"Psychological," I say.

A glass into the second bottle I go to the bathroom and he laughs at my face when I return. The toilets are Turkish, and he hasn't told me for his pleasure at this very moment.

I shrug. I have spent the three previous years squatting to pee in between parked cars and on the trunks of trees in New York; I do just fine balancing. The difficulty was when I came out of the bathroom and washed my hands at the shared sink. After I shook them off, the towels depleted, a man, far older than Andrew and drunker then either of us would be on that evening, leaned over and put his lips on my neck. I pushed him away with both arms, creating space between our bodies, as if he had fallen onto me by accident, but there was nothing accidental about that night, not for this man, or for me, or for Andrew, whom I part from on the Metro, pretending I am meeting up with friends for dinner when I just want to eat alone, to be alone with my body, which would, that year, always be more interesting to other people than it would be to me.

Sam, my American, sends me packages from his college in Minnesota. They arrive at the university's student center, and I open them alone, at lunch or on the Metro. He sends photos, silly ones, to make me laugh. At first, they have his arm in them as he holds the camera up; eventually, he gets other people to take them for him. All I can see is that these are the ones I have not taken, that his life is no longer mine, no longer ours. In early December, I'll get a photo of him standing on a snowdrift, shirtless. I put it on the wall above my bed, next to an old one of us in Central Park, where I set up my camera on a stack of our things late last spring. He covered me with his body in the grass—my teeth are bared, and he calls it the wild dog photo. *You are the dog,* I wrote on the back of his copy, which he keeps I don't know where.

Jamie I help move twice that year in Paris. I buy him cigarettes, hold them for him, lit, so he can zip up a jacket or pay a taxi driver. When he pays for my drinks I tell him I'm not going to sleep with him and he says, as he clinks our glasses together, "That's okay; you're still my favorite." The girls who do sleep with him are about my age but seem younger: debutantes and suburbanites who, the first time loose in a city, are always falling down stairways and yelling in the streets at 2:00 A.M., in English. Jamie, with his impeccable French, honed at an American boarding school, endures them for a few weeks at a time, collecting them like prizes, each one more beautiful than the last.

When he leaves one of these girls for the night, he calls me. Sometimes he is nearby and he's run out of money for a cab; sometimes he pretends he's locked himself out of his apartment again. He makes a pile of his smoky clothes in the front room. I let him into my bed; I let him lie against my back.

"So strong," he says, approvingly, as I try to unlace his fingers from mine, each of us protesting, half-asleep.

"Come on now," he pleads.

"Sleep," I tell him, and he does. We do.

When I wake up, we're not holding hands anymore. He leaves as if he has someplace to be, pinching me to let me know he is going. "I know you're trying to get me to bite you," I say, still in bed, "but it won't work."

When he leaves I open my two small windows to get the smoke smell out of the room.

Oliver writes me notes in books he's had sent from America or buys for me from Shakespeare and Company days after we discuss them. *Thought of you,* he'll write, or he'll copy a quote about friendship, about Paris, about the places we're from. He has the most beautiful handwriting I've ever seen, full of so much care. He never tries to stay the night. He never buys me wine, though I suspect his family is rich, a fact he hides from me by pretending money is nothing at all to him, handing me a roll of film he claims is about to go bad if it isn't used soon. "I over-ordered again," he says.

On Wednesdays we have a two-hour city walk as part of our Advanced Photography class. I passed over the more familiar options in the States for the school's competitive, yearlong photography courses, for the reputation of our professor, Peter Lincoln, as rigorous, as a career maker.

Oliver and I meet every week at the same *tabac* beforehand. Two years ahead of me in school, in Parisian life, he orders a coffee for me the way I can't seem to do correctly myself, the only way I can drink it without making a sour face.

The November day is gray and flat but I walk in wearing sunglasses. My hair is still wet, coiled in a rubber band at the base of my neck. I've forgotten a scarf; I don't own a hat.

"Night out with Jamie?" Oliver says when he notices me, and points to the coffee he has waiting for me on the bar. I push my sunglasses up off my face and take a sip of my coffee. He smirks. "Those first-year boys are always a little wild. Thought you'd have learned that by now."

It hurts to speak back but I have to. "I'm fine."

"Wait till we start walking," he says.

I groan. Peter is a notoriously fast walker; he waits for no one. My stomach turns at the prospect of keeping up. Oliver rubs my shoulder in a brotherly way and says we'd better get going.

Of the photos I end up taking that day, all Peter will say is, "Put something alive in it!" as if he's searched so hard for the words and is only now finding them, as if they are only for me, when he says this to someone at least once a week. At my midterm critique, he directs the other students through my work as quickly as possible; he doesn't like me, doesn't understand the work I'm making, but neither do I.

Oliver and Peter go out drinking together some afternoons. I should come along, Oliver suggests repeatedly, wanting to change both of our minds. I refuse.

"We don't connect," I say back, and count the weeks till the semester ends, till I can go home for winter break.

"You could, like, maybe not roll your eyes at him," Oliver says.

"He doesn't see me doing that."

"He knows."

"It's okay," I tell him. And for once I don't care whether the professor likes me, if I'm pleasant, or easy to teach, whether my work is any good.


Jean-Luc is perhaps married and definitely older but not American. On the day after Thanksgiving, which I have spent alone for the first time ever, he buys me a coffee and insists Sam is cheating on me back home. He insists on my youth and my naïveté and my future alignment with his truths. We spend four hours together before I remember that I can just get up and go.

I don't know a lot of women in Paris. They seem to be from another life of mine, and when I transfer to a college in California the next year I'll be hungry for them but I'll have forgotten how to be around them. It will take years to understand the different things that women want from me than men do.

Ilana, Oliver's ex-girlfriend, is a cocktail waitress at a bar we go to sometimes. For twenty-five francs, she will pour a shot of tequila into your mouth from her holster and pretend to like it. She does this wearing spandex shorts and a leather bra that matches the holster. "Would you ever?" he asks me, knowing no, I would not.

I'm afraid of her, more so when she is fully clothed, her knees bent to her chest while sitting on someone's floor at a party in the 11th, in an attic apartment with sloped ceilings. I have yet to meet anyone here who does not live under slanted walls. In this city, we all live in garrets.

Ilana is a dancer, and her body is something she uses to paint a scene, I hear her explain to a semicircle of our acquaintances, but not to me. She's never spoken to me. The scene in the bar pays her bills, she says, and "I don't give a fuck what you think of it."

Jamie and I talk about sex, generally, but in detail, as if our bodies are parts of a radio, or instruments we're both learning how to play. Strings. Him, a violin. Me, a guitar, a harp, a stand-up bass, maybe. I don't blush, don't think of him doing to me what he's describing doing to Rebecca, who is studying abroad from Tulane, who screams in bed so loudly the neighbors bang on the walls. He puts his hand over her mouth—"I think she kind of likes it," he says, and I roll my eyes and say, "Of course she does. It's a performance."

I feed him bits of my and Sam's sex life, never talking about him by name, as if there is anyone else I have loved in this way. I am only eighteen.

"It's simple," I say to Jamie over and over again, about what makes two people good together in bed, the talk becoming another kind of study for us, a working theory of pleasure. "Trust." I'm on his bed in his latest apartment, but sideways, and my shoes are still on. I am waiting for the Metro to reopen, trying not to fall asleep.

"Wanting," he says, "and then still wanting it. Take off your shoes already, will you?" he says, and kicks the soles of my boots.


Sam comes to see me in February, when it is dark and wet and flights are cheap. He has no French, no real interest in exploring the city, which I don't know how to show him; my list of places belongs to the other boys who have been showing it to me. I can't seem to find a corner of Paris that he would care about. He wants to stay in, anyway.

"I'm here to see you, for you," he says, trying to be tender, but by then, day five, neither of us is able to hide our mutual feelings of failure at how to be with each other here. We get too drunk; we fight. He calls me ungrateful; I tell him, on the steps of Montmartre, that his life is so much easier than mine, and always will be, to which he holds his arms out to the city I have decided I hate. Later that night, I bury myself in the familiar hollow of his collarbones, trying to figure out how he can still smell the same, how that smell draws a wet tang into my mouth. The sex that week is a poor antidote to our months of wanting, the pressure of its significance relieved only by getting my period the last two days of the visit. I stain through to the mattress that comes with my rented apartment.

When Sam leaves, I skip three days of classes. The day I go back, Jamie is outside the small building on a smoke break. Without even saying my name, he puts me under his arm like I am his, tells me we are going out that night whether I want to or not. Andrew, at the same bar, doesn't even look at me. I've dropped the lit classes this term; I wasn't pulling the grades I needed to transfer back to a college in the States.

"Don't be sad," Jamie says, tapping his pint glass gently against mine. "Be fun Anna."

"But you like the sad Anna," I say.

Before he's even drunk, he makes the offer to sleep with me, as he has so many times before, as he will continue to do till we're not speaking at all.

"Anytime you want," he says, his hand on my elbow in the way it often was that year, in a way that made me seem, to the other men around us, taken.

"Noted."

"I'm serious."

"I know," I say, and touch his face because it's right there.

The next morning, Jamie breaks my window by accident, a broken latch and our hangovers. He gets cut, but not so deeply he needs stitches. We ruin some towels cleaning him up. We do this together, a silent teamwork in which neither of us takes or places blame. It doesn't even seem funny, or that it could be, but it becomes that, a story we tell each other, though I don't know what makes us recall it at various times. We don't tell it to anyone else because it's always just the two of us; we don't like or understand each other's friends, don't need them. It's just us. We are an echo chamber.

Jamie doesn't offer to pay for any part of the window. When my landlady threatens to end my lease, Oliver says he will cover it, but I refuse. I overdraw my bank account again. Jamie never apologizes but I never expect him to.

That spring in Paris, I carry my camera in my backpack but most days I don't take it out. When I do, it does little to help me forget where I am. I don't turn it on myself, till one day I start setting the timer, arranging the camera on a chair, or a low wall, or a café table as I stare into the lens from above.

"What's the story?" Peter asks me after looking at my contact sheet.

I shrug. He taps the loupe against the table's surface loudly. "Anna, Anna. Try."

"I am," I say.

"Well then print whatever," he says, and walks across the room to another student.

The girl working across from me avoids my eyes, blushes as

I don't. It isn't time to leave the lab yet, and I bend over the sheet again, looking for one I can print, one that will prove Peter wrong. My hand shakes as I shift the loupe. I want to smash it against the classroom floor, but it's stronger than I am; the shards of glass would be so small, besides. I think of Jamie a few nights before, his bandaged hand in his pocket as we walked to his apartment with dinner: wine and bread and steaks he'd bought with a credit card he wasn't supposed to be using.

"You don't ever lie, do you?" he'd asked, implying an ease to my life, to have always appeared as I am, guileless, without needing to hide or change myself.

"Sure I do," I said, but he's a man, and the lies I'd told wouldn't register as big enough.

Peter always warned us against waiting for the story to appear through the loupe. "Know when you shoot," he'd say. I pretended I didn't know what the story was. There's something about me at that age that is trustworthy, that makes men think I will not judge them, though I do, all the time; I just keep it to myself. I am not beautiful, but I am pretty enough. That year, and for years after, I hold on to the pretty parts, to the appearance of being open. If only I had allowed myself to look mean in those photos.

On that day, I don't wait for Oliver like I usually do after class. I leave while he is still in the darkroom.

He's heard what happened. He finds me in the café that is our student center, and as he takes the chair across from mine he says, "He's pushing you." Oliver's work is thriving, but I am, I was told, wasting film. I am passing time.

"Do you want me to look?" he offers. I give him my contact sheet.

"This is so different than your other stuff," he says.

"The birds?" Earlier this year, I'd taken roll after roll of birds invading the parks.

"The New York stuff," he says.

Those photos got me into this class. I'd always been book smart, but photography was the thing that made me happiest, what I thought I wanted to pursue.

"Dead inside now," I say, and thud my heart with my fist.

"That's not what I meant," he says, annoyed. He taps the top right corner. "This one's good," he says, and hands me the sheet back. I don't print it.


When Jamie says to me, "I will not participate in breaking my own heart," what am I supposed to say?

It's the middle of the night, and we are both sober. We sit side by side on my bed. I don't want him to go. I could say his name; I could touch his knee. I could lie down next to him the way we have been all year when the loneliness gets to be too much. It's April; we're at the border of how hard I will try not to love him. I don't want him; I've waited all year for want to come to me so I don't have to think, but I think and think all year long and all it gives me is a series of near-mistakes I'm not smart enough to make. Those last few months in Paris nothing gets better, not my grades, or my photography, or the ache to return to a place I already know won't feel like home anymore.

That night, it's Jamie who takes one of my hands and wraps it in his, squeezing so hard it hurts a little.

Instead of saying ow, I tell him I'm sorry. I wasn't actually sorry. I lie, and he takes it, big enough for him at last. He kisses me on both cheeks, this French habit we've both affected, and he goes, forever.

Two months later, back in New York for the summer, I read the first of Oliver's letters with Sam's arm around my shoulders. He's shirtless, tan already, late June. The Paris postmark on the envelope makes me lonesome, a feeling I then understand will follow me wherever I am.

"Which one was he?" Sam asks as he scans the movie listings. We're in his family's apartment; we both have the night off from work.

"The one with the dancer ex. They're back together again, apparently."

I write Oliver back, apologizing for my handwriting. I tell him I miss him, but not Paris, that it's a shame he's fallen for it like every other sucker out there.

In July, I ask Sam to slap me while we're having sex, but he won't do it. It happens one night when we are both drunk after a party thrown by one of his new friends, on a week when we finally seem to be getting along again. I put his palm against my cheek. "There," I say. "No," he says. He slows down inside me but doesn't stop.

The next morning Sam pretends nothing happened. His year away from me has made him more beautiful: his jaw sharper, his body leaner and looser. He lifts me onto beds; his hands are strong, greedy for me in a way that should make me feel like I can't want anything or anyone else. In a month, he'll say that he has been worried about me all summer, that I am different. "Here I am," I'll tell him, repeatedly, sarcastically, unsure what else to offer him. He doesn't want to talk about what the year was like, how all my friends were men who didn't want to meet him when he came to visit, how I haven't reloaded my camera since I got home.

I never ask Sam to slap me again. I still wonder what it would have felt like, why other people like that sort of thing, but I never want it from anyone else.

I'm living in California when the last letter from Oliver comes. Peter's set him up with a good assistant job in New York. Oliver writes about how he proposed to Ilana while they were living there together, how she said no, how they are over for good. He asks if I've ever gotten around to reading the Barthes, what I thought of it. *Camera Lucida*, in its original French. Inside, he'd written: *You can handle it, A.* But I sold it, along with the other books he bought me, to Shakespeare and Company before I left. I needed the money, and besides, they would have been too heavy, too expensive to ship back. I no longer shoot on film, or take many photographs at all. I've forgotten too much, or maybe I just refused to learn it.

# Window Guards

The first time Owen shows me the photograph of the ghost dog, I don't believe it. "That's a toy," I say, but I don't laugh at him.

I'm sitting in the desk chair in his room. He stands behind me, all the ghost photos laid out on top of his chemistry textbook. He has about fifteen of these photographs—and some of them, I will grant him, are ghostly, but they are not ghosts. It's as though he's never seen a photograph before.

"No," he says, doubtless.

"It's stiff as a board," I say, and wait for him to say back, "Light as a feather," to use the language that keeps us tied to childhoods that, every day, feel further behind us than we want them to be. Next year, college.

He reaches over me and picks up the turn-of-the-century photograph of a girl, no older than five, holding a blur of a toy dog between her fat little hands. The photo is a series of grayscale curves: her perfectly parted hair, the curls they created to frame her round cheeks, the skirt of her dress. The lines of white in the middle of the photo ruin the composition; her eyes are sharp and bright at this understanding of what she's done. How long they must've asked her to hold still. So she shook the dog. Who wouldn't?

Owen goes nearly nose-to-nose with this girl, so unlike me: plump and angry and rich.

"It's the film," I say, and start to explain how the developing process works, how f-stops and reflections are all possible reasons for the white mass, but then he tosses the photo back onto the pile and crouches next to me. Lately, Owen avoids the packs of neighborhood boys, loud and careless, that we've grown up with; something has been ruined between them. After school, he looks for me. We watch movies and go on what he calls hikes but are really long walks through the parks in this northern part of the city. Sometimes, when we are alone, we make out, but the kissing—and that's all it is, for now—is just a comfort, an easy place to slip in and out of in the darkening afternoons.

Who cares, I think, as Owen presses his forehead against mine, whether he believes in ghosts? I still have my father's discarded hospital bracelets in a drawer, so who am I to say what is right to collect, to keep?

Owen's brother, Adam, was twenty-three when he disappeared. For months, people say they have seen him on the park peninsula, flat on his back on a bench, asleep, and when he is not, wide-eyed and silent, his face smudged or clean or looking older, or younger. No one can decide. Dominic says yes, he carries around an aluminum baseball bat; he must have found it near the batting cages. Kira says she saw him jogging, his knees dirty, his eyes distant but focused.

The last time I saw Adam myself, at their apartment six months ago, he asked Owen, "That your girl?"

"It's Lexie," Owen said to Adam, who squinted at me, and grinned when he seemed to square me, the girl before him, with whoever Lexie was to him. Maybe it had been a good number of months. Maybe I did look different from the girl in his mind who'd been friends with his brother since preschool.

Adam sat on a windowsill in the living room. It was March, and the window was open. The air was a touch cold still, but he wore short sleeves; the bandage from the IV insertion point from his latest trip to the psych ward, a few days earlier, was visible. Adam slapped a beat on his thighs; he played the drums, once, but this was sloppy, incoherent, and I watched Owen flinch at each strike.

Adam had tried to push Owen out of this same window a few weeks before, after Owen had thrown his headphones into the tree below it. They'd always thrown things into this particular tree—bags of trash, old clothes, water balloons—just because they could, because they were stupid, boys. The headphones were broken, and in the past, Adam would have laughed, too, even if he would also strike back. Owen would have shown me some little bruise, something moon shaped he'd pretend didn't bother him, but this time had been different. This time, the bruise Adam left was on Owen's neck. The window guards should have been taken out years ago, the brothers long past ten years old, the age at which the city stops requiring them, but they were, for whatever reason, still in.

"Lexie, Lexie, Leexxxxxieeee," Adam started to sing, out of rhythm. He wouldn't drop my gaze.

Adam had been, before this, beautiful, but on that day I began to wonder if that beauty wasn't something else, if that thing that Kira always called sexy (with a little moan for dramatic effect), was the start of his illness, a growing wild inside him.

"Let's go," Owen said to me.

Even as Adam's body was clumsy and slow from his new medications, his mind still understood Owen's weaknesses.

That was the first day, in the thirteen years I had known him, that Owen took my hand. We went to my apartment, where I kissed him over and over again, being careful of his neck.

Adam disappeared two months after that.

When our friends say they've seen Adam: with a drum, with a fifth of Crown, with a tiny white dog who sleeps curled behind his knees, Owen says no, he is gone.

# The Holographic Soul

We do the psychic trick for the new boys in the neighborhood in Louisa Phelps's backyard. It is the tipping point of June, the afternoon before the last day of school, and the heat has already settled in, bringing the bees, which buzz near our unshod toes. Louisa's backyard is between the new boys' and ours, and when our father looks at V and me sternly enough, we play over there, although it is clear Louisa doesn't like either of us very much. But today she's willing to play any game; the presence of new kids gives her a chance not to be despised and ignored as the ineffective tyrant she is.

I am the transmitter, V is the receiver. Louisa, restrained in her better self, lets the boys be our subjects. Aaron, who will be in my class in the fall, cups his hands over my ear without actually touching it and whispers to me in a slow Midwestern accent. At the edge of the yard, my sister suspends herself by her knees from a low tree branch until we call her back to us.

V arranges herself on the grass in between Aaron and his younger brother, Charlie, closing the circle we have created. She shuts her eyes, and then I shut mine, occasionally peeking through my eyelashes. Everyone giggles, then quiets. I can hear the boys breathing, leaning in, Louisa's fingers tapping her sandals. We make them wait a good two minutes before I open my eyes and start to ask V questions.

"Is it a loaf of bread?"

"No." V's dark eyebrows furrow, two smudge marks of smoke.

"Is it a school bus?"

"No."

"A roller coaster?"

V's eyes roll around in her head, her hands rattle ever so slightly—a new touch. "Nuh-uh," she says, letting disappointment cross her face.

"A bookmark?"

"Really now, Hannah. Concentrate, please." V's exasperation is part of the act.

"A motorcycle?"

"Nope."

"A banana split?"

V licks her lips. "Yum. Yes."

The boys' mouths open into skeptical o's of disbelief. Their eyes narrow. They call us lucky. The three Yarrow girls come by with their little brother; Louisa's sisters come home from high school. They make us prove ourselves again and again, have us switch roles, turn our backs on one another, be blindfolded with a scarf Louisa retrieves from her mother's dresser drawer. They guess at tricks of counting, hand signals, a hidden mirror.

"We're just psychic," says V.

"No, you're not," says Louisa, standing. She tosses her doll-like corn-silk hair over her shoulder. She is a year older than I am, but I want to yank it. "You're just liars."

V shrugs; I take a moment to pick the grass off my knees. We wouldn't reveal our secret under torture, or call them jealous, though they must be; V and I are the only siblings in the neighborhood who don't try to leave each other at home, or sacrifice each other during the backyard games that always end in someone else's tears. V and I need only each other.

Earlier today I looked in on V at school. We are just a grade apart, and because Mrs. Martin keeps her classroom door open, I can see V bent over her desk by the window whenever I pass through the fifth-grade hallway on my way to the bathroom, her misaligned grip on the pencil, her ponytail crooked and sinking with the weight of her hair. Finding my sister in the room has become a ritual for me, knowing she is okay, even though I have no reason to believe she isn't. I will be across the street in junior high next year, and my last glance at V finds her as she always is, how I want her always to be in my mind.

In Louisa's yard, my little sister stands and points her chin up to meet Louisa's glare. V smiles at her sadly, as if Louisa were the littlest kid there, the dumb one in the class. "We were born this way," she says, and hooks her elbow through mine before we turn toward home.

Dad started running this spring. Every night at 5:45, four or five men gather by our house, which sits at a central corner in the neighborhood. The runs last till dinnertime, when each man splits off into his own driveway, nodding his good-bye. Afterward, our father stands in our kitchen proudly, his hair, dark and thick like ours, glistening with sweat. He picks out half-cooked vegetables from the skillet over our mother's shoulder until she swats at him with a wooden spoon and tells him to shower already. She uses a tone not unlike the one she uses with us when we wait for attention too long.

When we come home this evening, Mr. Keller is outside with Dad, both of them stretching against the yellow clapboard.

"Well, well, well, if it isn't the amazing Oliver sisters," Mr. Keller says as we approach, and this lights us up, as if he knows what we have just been doing, as if he knows of our small triumph.

"You girls meet the new boys yet?" Mr. Keller asks us. Then he leans into Dad, says, "Interesting guy. Hedge funds. Chicago," and Dad raises his eyebrows in agreement.

"Whaddaya think, Vanessa?" Mr. Keller bends down to V as though he were talking to the Litmans' new puppy. "Think they'll be okay? Should we let them in?" Our neighborhood is known for girls. Mr. Keller has four of them, all older; two were our babysitters till last year, when we were allowed to be at home by ourselves.

Dad does an eye roll for our benefit behind Mr. Keller's back.

"Yeah, sure, whatever," V says with a shrug. Her arm is still absently hooked through mine—she often forgets her limbs, as if they weren't attached to her own body—and our shoulders lift together, conjoined twins.

When Mr. Heineman and Mr. Phelps come, the men take

off. We watch the pack of fathers disappearing down the road in their white T-shirts and blue shorts, an unacknowledged and accidental uniform, and after a few hundred yards it is hard to tell which one is ours.

Inside, a note on the kitchen table reads: *Girls, At the grocery. If client comes early, stall.—M.* My mother has the whole day to go to the supermarket, but she likes to go at five o'clock, to pull into a crowded parking lot with all the other people who've just remembered they have to cook dinner. She says that having to constantly move her cart out of the way keeps her in touch with the normal folks, but her face puckers on the word *normal* as though it were a joke.

When asked, our mother will say she was a photojournalist, and pause before tacking on a "once." At those moments, my father will note that she takes stunning portraits, and my mother will make some huffing noise and mumble about famous people and their vanity. Now her work is mostly head shots. Even though she works from home, she's always late for her appointments, no matter how famous the clients. "Another writer," she remarked about tonight's shoot to my father over the phone earlier, and then he said something that made her laugh.

The writer knocks on our front door ten minutes early. I walk him back to the studio; V follows, jumping from stone to stone along the path that connects it to the house. The studio used to be the garage. My father had the renovations done two summers ago while my mother was on a monthlong assignment in Tel Aviv, her last travel assignment, and V and I were at sleepaway camp and hating it. He went a little overboard, installing revolving walls and electronic shades and built-in speakers. My mother is always losing the remotes for what she calls the "contraptions." The back half of the studio is a darkroom, accessible through two sets of doors, each one triggering the lights on or off. We glow orange in there; V's chunks of black hair become inkier, and her eyebrows stand out, like they might march right off her face. We are not allowed in much, partly because Mom doesn't want us around the chemicals, which drip from the tongs and sinks, which she says will make her go mad, eventually, and partly because she says we get in her space—the darkroom's built for one, my father will say, in a tone that is meant to soften the blow.

The skylights are open in the studio today, and the floor blazes white beneath us. I lead the writer to a chair that looks out over the garden.

"You two twins?" the writer asks me while V gets him a bottle of water from the mini-fridge.

"No, I'm older," I say.

"I'm the older one, too," he says, taking off his blazer and hanging it neatly over his chair. There are ovals of dampness under his arms. Besides this, he is sort of handsome for an older person, because he looks not unlike Indigo Roberts, in the seventh grade, how Indigo might look when he gets taller and starts to dress more seriously.

"What's your book about?" I ask, while V wanders the room poking at all the things Mom wouldn't want her to touch.

"Your mother and I have a lot in common, actually. I cover the same places in Africa she photographed for her book."

Before she met my father, before she had us, my mother published a book, a famous book, of photographs of children in Sudan. *The Disinherited* was published thirteen years ago, while my mother was pregnant with me.

"She doesn't really do that stuff anymore," I tell him. She hasn't taken a foreign assignment since the studio went up.

"I see." He smiles at me before screwing the cap back on the bottle after a gulp of water.

"We're psychic, you know," V says, appearing suddenly between us.

"Vanessa," I warn. Usually we don't offer the trick to adults—they all assume we're lying, and so they fake belief; their playing along is worse than anything we could be accused of by our peers.

"It's true," V says, lowering her voice. "Hannah's just embarrassed. Doesn't want us to get too in demand."

"You work as a team, huh?" He looks from her to me, his smile asking whether I am in on this game or not.

I want to say no, but I can't. I don't know what has gotten into her; she stands with her hands on her hips, her face showing the same sense of victory Dad's shows in the kitchen after his runs.

"Oh yeah. You have to tell her something," V says, indicating me with her head. "A word or a name or something. I'll leave the room if you want."

I am saved by the sound of a car door closing.

"That's Mom," I say.

"Maybe another time," he says, winking at me when V turns to look out the window to make sure.

Our mother comes in full of apologies and smiles—when

she wants, her face can make anyone feel loved, special. She hands V the car keys; it's her week to unload the groceries. V groans but marches off to the car dutifully. When Mom goes to shake the writer's hand, she looks old next to him; I realize they are different degrees of adult.

"It's such a pleasure to meet you," the writer says, rising to greet her. "I'm a huge fan of your work."

"And you, Mr. Kingsley, as well. I've been following your series in the *Times*. I hear it's been causing just the right amount of trouble."

"Call me Robert, please." He watches Mom as she unpacks her equipment. "You're very kind, as are your daughters. Vanessa was just telling me about their special ability."

My mother pauses in assembling a light kit behind him. "Oh, and what's that?" She looks at me, a frozen smile masking a kind of worry.

"Nothing, just a game."

She looks between us. "I hope they didn't—"

"No, no, they are lovely. Very hospitable," he says, and winks at me again.

"Why don't you go help your sister unpack?" Mom says to me, her chin pointing me toward the doors. As I leave, she gives her hair a good shake before pulling it back into a fresh ponytail, as though she's sliding off one face for another. She steps in front of the writer. "We ready?"


I have trouble falling asleep, and while V yelps in her sleep like a puppy, I slip out of our bedroom and into the hall. The stairs creak under my feet, but no one wakes, and I wander into the study, stand in front of the shelves that hold my mother's collection of photography books. *The Hollywood Starlets of the 1940s* is my favorite—the old shots of Veronica Lake's hair cascading over her right brow, a curtain behind which she hid. But tonight I reach for *The Disinherited*, which I haven't looked through in years.

My mother's photographs of the orphans are in black and white, crisp and glowing at the edges with gray light. The orphans' feet are bare and their eyes are bright against the blackness of their skin. When I was younger and home sick from school, Mom used to turn the pages with me, stroking my hair and telling me the boys' names—Santino, Saloua, Maduk—but I've long since forgotten the stories she told me about each boy. She said then that the orphans project was what made her want to have children. When I touched the orphans' faces in the book, I felt connected to them; I thought that this was somehow where we came from. I thought about how much luckier we were, V and I.

But tonight I feel something else when I touch them. As the old clock in the study clicks over toward midnight, I think of the blush of Mr. Kingsley's face when my mother complimented him, how they lingered after the appointment, talking in serious tones, his card between her solution-stained fingers. V and I were out in the yard, snipping basil for dinner, which Dad had started in the kitchen. V was going on about how Louisa made her blood boil, and didn't notice a thing. I touch the orphans' faces and think of my mother's this afternoon—how for a moment when I saw her in the studio doorway, I didn't recognize it. A pit opens in my stomach.

School ends on a half day. We have a party in our class, and the little kids watch our graduation ceremony—mock, since we are only moving to another building. At the end of the day, our knapsacks still hold the shape of our returned textbooks; we fill them with that year's art and papers and walk home with their lightness at our backs.

To celebrate, V and I decide to lie in the backyard in our bathing suits, our freshly washed beach towels side by side, but neither of us lasts very long. Bees collect on our sandwich crusts; it's hot, our sprinkler is broken, and though Louisa's might work, we don't think we'd be welcome over there today, after the mind-reading business. We wander into the house in our suits, where our father is packing for a business trip to Brazil. My parents' bedroom is shady and cool; we sit on the edge of the bed, next to the half-filled suitcase.

"How long will you be gone?" I ask.

"Two weeks."

"What are you going to do there this time?" V wants to know, as if we ever comprehend what he tells us about his work. An econ geek, our mother calls him, even though anyone can see it isn't so; my father is so handsome, completely in command of himself.

"You know, spying, drinking, the usual."

My father was an economist with the foreign service when

he met my mother in Africa. After my parents had me, he left the service to work for a consulting firm. When we were kids, he told us he was a spy and swore us to secrecy.

"Great," says V, continuing their routine, "don't forget to send a postcard."

"I won't," he says, ruffling her hair, perfectly earnest. He searches the room for the one thing he's forgotten, but doesn't find it. He shuts the case and kisses each of us good-bye, twice.

While our father's plane hurtles toward Rio de Janeiro, my mother takes a series of calls on her studio phone, pacing the floor in bare feet and old jeans, while V and I wait for dinner; we always go out on the nights Dad leaves. We open the cabinets in search of something to snack on, but each door reveals disappointment: high-fiber cereal, enough cans of stewed tomatoes to drown the neighborhood, expired granola bars. My mother's trips to the store are habitual, not necessary, and she forgets to check the inventory.

At seven o'clock, V makes a sign that reads, WE'RE HUNGRY!!!!!! and holds it against the glass of the studio doors. Mom holds up two fingers and mouths "soon" to us. When she gets off the phone, she's in such a good mood she lets us pick whatever restaurant we want for dinner.

Mom has her portfolio under her arm when she leaves for her appointment the next day. She puts ten dollars for lunch under our library cards. V is antsy and excited, which is odd, because she hates the library, hates to read or sit still. "You lead," she says to me as we walk our bikes from the shed in the backyard, where we keep them. Usually she wants to lead, and we battle over the position for a few minutes, deliberately misremembering who was in charge of our route last time we went out. I pick the downhill routes for some breeze, but we are both sticky by the time we get there. Our black curls are too short to stay put behind the rubber bands of our ponytails; they drop sweat onto our foreheads.

"I wish we belonged to a pool," I say as we dismount. Our parents have refused, not because of money, but because they think it is an idle way to spend a summer, lying around on wet towels, eating snack bar french fries.

"Uh-huh," V says as she hastily locks our bikes up together and rushes into the cool of the building. She is acting indifferent, but I know she would like the pool as much as I would.

I watch her walk through the turnstile into the tall stacks of the adult section, which we have never entered. She looks both ways as if crossing a street and decides to go left.

I feel like a baby among the low tables and primary-colored furniture of the children's section, even though the books run all the way up to teen, which seems light-years away, even if I will be twelve at summer's end. I pick out two Betsy-Tacy books, and when I go to the checkout, V is waiting for me on the other side of the counter. Her head is propped on her arms, two books under her elbows, the fluorescent lights shining a glare on their plastic-coated covers.

I carry V's library card with mine; she is always losing it. I pass the card over to the librarian who checks me out. "It's for her," I say, pointing to my sister, on the other side. "That's her card."

The librarian pauses over V's books and can't suppress a snide smile as she stamps them with the return date. V grabs the books off the desk without a thank-you, shoving them under her arm. She's not dumb; she can see what the librarian thinks.

"Idiot," she says, glaring at the library doors as she hands me her books—*Getting in Touch with the Other Side* and *Awakening the Psychic Within*—to put in my backpack. I should reprimand her for not bringing her own bag, tell her that their weight will make my back stickier, but she's already in a foul enough mood. She swings up her kickstand forcefully.

"Go," she says, waiting for me to lead again.

We ride home in silence. At the house, V becomes so immersed in her books that she spends the afternoon behind their covers; I don't see her till dinnertime, after which she again disappears to our room, taking the last red Popsicle with her.

When I get into bed, she is still reading, her lips puckering in concentration. I can't recall the last time I saw her so serious.

"What are you learning?" I ask quietly, turning on my bedside lamp.

"That I don't need you to do it."

"What do you mean?" A wave of warmth spreads up my back. I push the thin cotton blanket to my knees.

"Only one of us has to be psychic. It's not about how connected we are to each other, but about tuning in to the universe, to your instincts."

"Oh?" I'm trying not to laugh, to not be on the side of the librarian, but I stifle a smile. V is too absorbed in her reading to notice. I try to read, too, but I'm burning with heat and can't concentrate on Betsy and Tacy lacing up their ice skates. V has the same blankets as I do but she is perfectly still. I shift my feet out, push the blanket to my side.

"You hot?" she asks me without looking up.

"You psychic?"

"Probably."

Probably not, I think, but don't say. V hates to be ignored. Instead, I stare at the ceiling, trying to tire my eyes out by drawing imaginary circles on it.

"I might wake up," V tells me as she closes the book.

"Why?"

"I might have a vision in the middle of the night and have to write it down."

"Okay. Why are you telling me this?"

"I just want you to be prepared."

"Good night, V," I say, clicking off my light.

"Good night, Hannah."

She sleeps through the night soundly, as she always does, rooted to the mattress. I know because I am the light sleeper and wake several times from halfhearted dreams to see in the blue light of night her arm folded underneath her chin, where it stays till morning.

I steal the books from the top drawer of V's nightstand the next afternoon while she is at piano. The second half of *Getting in Touch with the Other Side* consists of exercises and projects, like in those how-to books Grandma Oliver always brings us on crocheting and bread baking and other hobbies we don't have. Number 17 has you write down your dreams. Number 6, an accelerated vision quest, requires two people. Skimming the chapters on precognition and channeling, I don't know why V would want to see such things: our dead relatives at the foot of her bed, the locations of children held hostage by torturers, car crashes and heart attacks before they happen. I think of the people who must have died in this house, and the possibility of them waiting for us to deliver messages for them gives me the shivers.

I switch to *Awakening the Psychic Within*. V's bookmark rests in a chapter called "The Holographic Soul." *All around the world, fragments of a shared Oversoul are embodied at the very same moment in the very same lifetime! These connected incarnations across space connect you to your holographic soul fragments throughout the world. Your soul fragments might be living as you live as a boy in Egypt or a girl in Chile or a set of brothers in Africa while also being embodied by you! This is your holographic soul absorbing the vast array of truths and pains and joys of human experience over a single lifetime. These other parts of your soul in other bodies are what some call Twin Flames, or more commonly, Twin Souls.*

V's highlighted a few lines in purple marker: *The only safe way to remain open to the possibilities of these truths and experiences is through your own soul group, preferably through fusing your energies with your Twin Flame or Soul Mate.* Next to this she's written *H???* in pencil.

As an afterthought that is clearly not, my mother ends the story of her and my father's time in Africa by saying she always wondered what it would have been like to adopt one of the orphans. So many of them were sent to the States in those days as a result of the attention her book drew. I imagine a tall African boy living in our bedroom instead of us, taking part in Louisa's backyard games, helping our father dig out his car in winter. I wonder, if V were really able to reach out and touch another person's soul, if this is who she'd get, the unfinished business of my mother's life.

Mom ruins our first dinner with Dad back in town by telling us Bob's invited her to do a follow-up project with him in Sudan. She'll be gone nearly three months. My father's tan from his trip to Brazil, but I can still see the nervous flush creeping up his neck when V starts to cry.

"Who's Bob?" V spits, infuriated.

"The writer, honey, Robert Kingsley. You met him a few weeks ago."

"You're going away with some guy you just met?"

"No, it's not like that," my mother says in a soothing tone, but V's breathing only gets heavier.

"We decided you girls are old enough for Mom to do some more traveling again," my father tries.

V looks at all of us accusingly before bolting up the stairs. She locks herself in our room, pressing her weight against the door to keep us out. I don't have to fight very hard to get inside, and when I do, shutting the door on my parents, who've followed me, she falls right into my arms. I let her hot tears collect in the dip of my collarbone, let her snot all over my neck. As she shakes against me, I realize that she never saw it coming, and I should have told her something; I should have let her in.

It's a surprise to see Louisa at our door a half hour later, winding her blond hair around her fingers with worry. Aaron hit his head at the pool, she explains. There was blood; it turned the water pink and the lifeguards blew their whistles and made everyone go home, before the ambulance even got there. Louisa says she saw it pull up as she left. I think I see tears in the corners of her eyes when she says, "A concussion," and then, in a whisper, "He's in the hospital. He has to stay up all night. So he doesn't die."

V, her eyes still puffy and raw, nods as though she already knows this, and steps outside.

"I just want him to be okay," Louisa says, and bends to scratch a mosquito bite on her left calf, I think to hide her despair. "Will you help?" She looks to us.

"Of course," my sister says before I can protest. In the falling evening light of our neighborhood, her hair glows like something holy.

She instructs Louisa to get something of Aaron's—the closer to him the better, so a piece of clothing or a possession would be ideal—and to meet us in her yard in half an hour.

"You want me to break into his house?" Louisa asks, her old self.

"Do you want him to pull through or not?" I ask.

I don't say anything to V as we load the dishwasher, don't ask what she plans on doing, just let her be in charge; I have a strange faith in her tonight, not because I think she'll do anything miraculous, but because I feel that I owe her my belief.

In Louisa's yard, V instructs us to put our hands on a half-deflated basketball Louisa swears Aaron touched the other day. Our fingers overlap on its dusty skin. V takes us through one of the exercises from *Getting in Touch with the Other Side*—or two, I can't tell. We all imagine Aaron as the strongest animal we can, then we walk with that animal through a field, to its home, which is full of fruit. In a lull, I begin to hum a little something, and V joins in, the tune she's been practicing in piano, just the few bars I know, over and over again. After a few rounds, we extend the last few notes, and let the silence sink in, let the crickets take over.

"Did you feel that?" V asks. "The universe shifting?"

"Yes," Louisa and I both answer.


The day after Mom leaves, Dad gives us pool passes at breakfast, as if it were a coincidence, but neither of us is above taking the bribe. "Just promise me you won't go running around like your neighbor the fool," he says, and knocks once on each of our skulls. He makes sure we put on sunscreen before we leave the house; V's hands impatiently smack it onto my back in a way I know will be uneven. He presses five-dollar bills into our palms and hands us each a hat, which we both shove to the bottom of our bags once we are outside. We are at the pool gates when the lifeguard unlatches them for the morning.

Aaron and Charlie show up with a babysitter around eleven. Excepting a little bit of hair shaved from where they put the stitches in, Aaron is walking and talking like the rest of us, and occasionally shoves Charlie's head underwater as they play catch with a foam football.

We spend most of the day in the water, our fingertips shriveling, our eyes burning from the combination of chlorine and sun. We climb out to get hot dogs and waffle fries, which we eat atop damp towels on a shared lounge chair, licking the salt from our bleached finger pads with joy.

On the way back from the bathroom, where we hovered over the salty-smelling toilets, our rubber flip-flops slipping in what we hoped was collected pool water underneath, V stops Aaron where he's just climbed out of the pool.

"Did you see it?" she asks him, staring right into his eyes.

"See what?"

"The light." V puts her hand to Aaron's wrist.

"The what?" He shivers at her touch, perhaps just from a girl touching his skin, or from the drops of pool water collecting on his shoulders. He doesn't have a towel.

"The light, the bright white one."

"You," he declares, "are weird," before propelling himself into the deep end.

Other mothers sit on chairs by the pool, resting a leg on the ground and keeping their eyes only half on their books, their whole bodies ready to make a save. When V and I float on our backs, I think of our mother, her love of the water; she's the one who taught us to swim. She'd stand in the shallow end and make a fortress around our bodies with hers, moving as we moved down the length of the pool, always letting us think we were still connected when we weren't.

I remember a family vacation we took to Florida a few years before, how happy Mom looked coming up from the Atlantic, how she held V by her waist as the ocean lifted and settled them down again and again. They were singing, their mouths open to the sky, but neither my father nor I could hear their song. We watched from a beach chair, my back up against his knees, burrowing our toes into the sand. His arms were slung over my shoulders. He whistled low and sweet, never taking his eyes off Mom or V. "Those two," he said then, and though he was laughing softly, there was a kind of sadness in his voice, too.

In the pool, I hear V breaking the water next to me, then feel her fingers tickling the sole of my foot. I flip over and see her underneath me, holding her back to the floor of the pool. Smiling a goofy smile, she shakes her shoulders in a mermaid's boogie.

Through that wavy, aqua light, in my bathing suit from last year, my sister looks to me the way she will look the first time I take her to the airport with an open-ended ticket to someplace she has to touch with her own two hands. She'll never outgrow the belief that there is something to see beyond this world. That first trip will be to India, but later it will be Vietnam, Iceland, Mali, Kenya, among others. Like my father, she'll always send postcards, which he says my mother reads to herself first before she repeats them aloud for him; he says she's always smiling when she does. The first time V goes, she is twenty; I am a fresh twenty-two, and my instincts will tell me it's a miracle we managed to hang on to her so long, though knowing that won't make it any easier to watch her shut the car door and load her pack onto her shoulders, to see her smile as she walks away from me, for me to start to learn how to pass the time with something other than worry. On the way home from the airport that day, I'll feel the faintest weight of her beside me in the passenger's seat, like a ghost waiting for a message we never learned how to deliver.

# Landscape No. 27

Remember when we hiked where we weren't supposed to? We missed a trail mark and didn't notice for a good half mile. The distance between the rocks got wider as we climbed higher, you in front, humming, and then not. I saw you thinking about turning around and offering your hand to me, but you knew I wouldn't take it, and neither of us wanted to say we had gone off course, because it would sound like a bad metaphor and the idea that it might be true was too much for either of us to admit.

And then you just stopped going forward, or sideways it was, really, at that point, both of us hugging the face of a boulder, the river a good two or three apartment stories beneath us. "I don't remember this," you said. I hadn't even seen the map. Once we were on the other side of the rope for the closed-off section we had ended up in, you tapped your knuckles against the sign that read: DANGEROUS! SLIDE AREA!

Neither of us slipped on our way down either, but by the time we got to your car at the trailhead, I couldn't stop shaking, the way I had after childbirth, a giddy involuntary convulsion, my body smarting at its survival. You wouldn't know this because you weren't there. You have no children, and we agreed early on not to talk about mine, to pretend my entire family didn't exist.

We sat in the open hatch of your car, smacking away the last of the bugs from the woods, my knees rattling, though you didn't notice. I had to show you a crazy smile that chattered and you gave me a look as if you hadn't been the one to insist we turn around. As you rubbed my shoulders, mistaking it for chills, I thought of my midwife cooing at the baby thirteen years ago, the boy, as she pushed my knees apart again and again so she could examine me, apologizing, both of us laughing. "Just a few stitches," she said, and promised I wouldn't feel them. I had no drugs in me, only adrenaline, more than my body knew what to do with. This was the way I wanted to feel when I was with you—my body running clear over my mind.

I have two kids, the boy and a girl, and neither of them likes to go hiking. Their labors were slow and long and mostly silent, which isn't a metaphor for anything. That morning my husband had kissed me good-bye so lightly it was as though we hadn't touched at all.

I have never worn a wedding ring and you never asked why. My husband and I couldn't afford rings at first, and later when we could, they still seemed an unnecessary expense. Neither of us would have bought into that kind of illusion anyway, had you invited me to your studio with one on my hand, had I had to remove it, or catch you looking at it, wondering what it meant.

In those days, I needed a secret. The sex was fine but not that exciting. After the first few times, it was just sex, just acts with bodies that felt good at the time. Different than with my husband, but it didn't tie me to either of you more or less. How simple that would have been, to have been driven by wanting. Led. One time in the shower you licked the water off my breast, and I thought your smile meant something interesting was still ahead for us, but then you complained about the taste of the water and asked me to go into the bedroom.

When I cut my hair you thought it was for you—you were always moving it off my neck because it fell in your face when I was on top of you. I loved my hair then: It was long and thick and the color of a honey jar on a sunny windowsill, and I liked it too much when you pulled it away, the grip of your hands, your assured possession of my body in that moment. When I came home from that haircut my husband said I looked cute, and kissed my newly exposed neck. This, too, was the first place you put your lips when you saw me next. The cut made my face look tired, serious. It reflected those hate-filled days. It gave you nothing to grab on to, my childish attempt to dull the pleasure I couldn't decide I wanted or deserved.

I was annoyed by the collective failure of your imagina- tions, by your inability to follow me into the hard place I was going with anything other than an offer to fuck me anyway. You both liked my hair better long; most men do. You want safety and familiarity as much as any of us. I've bought that bullshit of men's wildness, the story of your ease in recklessness, as much as anyone else. A painter, for chrissakes.

The second time we were together I didn't even need the

whiskey. We didn't bother flirting. Negotiations had ended when I sat on your couch a week before. In our five months together, I didn't have to lie, not once. My best friend saw your picture on your website and called you *yummy*, made some comment about me running away with you that was so far from possible in her mind that I didn't even blush as I made a bad joke about fucking you in paint.

That first day you took me up to your studio above the gallery, flipping the sign on the door so that it read BACK IN A BIT, you showed me the paintings that weren't for sale, the non-landscapes you said you were too afraid to market. You thought it might be confusing, and this is how you seemed to me, confused, even as you offered me a drink at two o'clock in the afternoon, as though it could mean anything else.

I calculated the hours till I had to pick up the kids from practice and after-school, some play my daughter was in that I kept forgetting the name of. I had three hours to kill, enough time to drink a whiskey and be sober enough to drive to get them half an hour away. I have always said yes more than I've said no. You were the first person in days to talk to me like I was a human being. I liked you.

I found this thing in my husband's T-shirt drawer, a long scrap of fabric, black and shiny, frayed at its edges. The kind of thing you could use to tie someone up, or pull through your hands when you miss them. I held it up to my nose, but it didn't smell like anything. It spanned the length of my arms. I had never seen it before, but we weren't in the habit of being in each other's things. I wanted it to mean something, something I didn't know or understand—someone, I hoped. The longer I hold on to that hope, the more I know it's nothing.

I have no photos of you, though you tried, so many times, to get me to send you photos of myself, of my body half-dressed—the way you must think of me, I guess, dressing and undressing. I didn't want to be careless, I said, but the truth is I didn't want you to own any piece of me and, well, as for those paintings of yours I bought, I gave away every last one of them, and we both know that they aren't as much a piece of you as the ones you won't sell. Maybe one day I will buy one of those.

And the most dangerous part of it all was not the drop into the river, not going into the woods with you alone, not how you held my hand when we walked the streets of a town where everyone knew you, but being on that ledge with a man I had no desire to understand at all. How little we cared to know each other, the protective distance we put between ourselves, filled with our bodies. Your skinny legs, my hair when it was long scattered in your sheets and no seduction in the daylight, not quite animal enough. Only now do I wonder what you were thinking, what put you on that ledge, what made you think to ask me, of all people, to go with you.

# Hide and Seek

The children are outlining each other's bodies with chalk in the driveway when their uncle's car pulls in. Magnolia pops up from the asphalt as soon as the car door opens. Pale purple chalk dusts the crown of her brown wavy hair, and green marks the insides of her fingers. Seven years old, she still greets Nick with a full-body throttle, screaming his name as he gathers his things from the backseat: a light long-sleeved shirt to keep the mosquitoes away on the August evening, beer for himself and his sister, the bag of charcoal she asked him to pick up from the store.

"Mag! I'm not done yet!" complains Sunshine, crouched before the misshapen, legless form her sister occupied a moment before.

Magnolia accepts a kiss from Nick pressed onto her cheek.

"Better get over there and finish what you started, huh? Hello, Sunny," he calls to the older one. "Where's your mom at?"

Of all the things he has learned to accept about his sister's life—her abandonment of Manhattan, her determination to raise her kids alone—the strange optimism of the girls' names is still hard to swallow. Sunshine and Magnolia, like rescued dogs, like hippies. Alison's the only one who insists on their full names; it's only Sunny who corrects her mother's introduction of her by it, for now.

"Did I ask you not to do that in the driveway or what?" Alison's voice comes from around the side of the house before she does. She gives Sunshine's earlobe a playful tug. "Can you believe these two?" she asks Nick as she motions toward the backyard.

The girls have switched places now, Sunshine holding the chalk hand of Magnolia's two-dimensional self, whose head she has decorated with her name in hasty blue lettering.

Alison watches Nick make room for the beers among the hot dog packs and tubs of coleslaw in the fridge. Usually, after his shifts at the police station, he will pick up a six-pack for what she's taken to calling their "bullshit in the backyard" sessions, but tonight he's brought two.

"Let's go outside," he says, uncapping their beers.

They sit in the lawn chairs on the stone patio, looking out into the backyards that face Alison's. There are no fences in this neighborhood, but the houses sit so deep back you'd need a megaphone for a neighbor to hear you. Out front, the girls take turns throwing a rubber ball against the garage door.

"You need to mow your lawn," Nick says. His fingers work

the beer bottle's label, the tiny bits of paper collecting on his shorts.

He's always on her about the upkeep on the house, a future problem he wonders if she's considered, the unspoken worry about how she will pay for what hasn't yet happened. Alison inherited the house from a great-aunt who gave a big screw-you to the rest of the family by leaving it to the distant niece who'd made all the questionable life choices. No one had imagined Alison would actually move the kids from Manhattan here, but she did. At least he's dropped the idea of them moving back into the building their parents still own on West Fifty-sixth, where they grew up. She's heard enough about how happy they'd be to take a hit on the market-rate rent to have her and the girls closer, as if the Bronx is another state.

Nick's never been good at hiding himself from his big sister. It's not unusual for his mind to be elsewhere after a shift, but tonight he looks at her with a heaviness that she knows means something worse than a bad day at work. She wishes it were about some girl; it never is.

"Nicholas," she says, sternly, jokingly. "Out with it." She doesn't want to wait all night for bad news.

"When the girls are asleep."

"Just say it."

He stands up and peeks down the side of the house that leads to the front, where the girls are shouting at each other about turns, on the verge of a fight. He sits back in the chair, puts his beer on the ground. "I got a call from downtown this morning. There was an incident a couple of days ago, on Twenty-first, by the river. Michael was stabbed."

"Oh?" Alison asks as if she hasn't been listening, as if the utterance of the name she has forbidden in her house is just a coincidence.

"He's dead," he says.

Alison puts a hand over her lower stomach, but it doesn't do anything to stop what feels like being on a tossing boat with the shore nowhere in sight.

"Okay," she says.

Nick shifts his weight on the old metal patio chair, its creaking filling the silence between them. "It's done, though. You don't have to do anything," he says after a bit.

A door closes somewhere in the house; small feet pound the stairs.

"Frank and Carrie?" Alison asks.

Michael's siblings, both of whom live crime-free, family-centered lives in Westchester, refused to come downtown, having, as Alison had, cut him off or lost him some time ago. Nick shakes his head.

Alison said her good-bye to Michael at twenty-five, when she was pregnant with Magnolia, a decade of his quick and selfish choices behind her. She asked him to leave them alone, and he listened, the way he had when she'd said she wanted to get married, have babies. Some days, Magnolia will lift her arm a certain way and Alison will lose her words, have to shake the image of his ghost, tamp down the fact of loving him, of having loved him, and of loving Magnolia now, in the moment of putting on her shirt or reaching for a light switch. She can't control when she sees him—this will never die—but she is grateful that at least the girls will never know whom they're tied to, that they belong to him, too. She will be the only one who knows the depth of that, who will see it. An apt punishment for the foolishness of her youth.

"I wasn't next of kin? For the body?"

"You wouldn't have wanted to do that," Nick says.

He's right; she's relieved to have been spared the question, but she won't thank him for it. She stands, her now-empty bottle in her hands. "Want another one?"


The house is under-furnished and cavernous, too much space for a single mother and two little girls. While it would make sense for Alison to sell the house, to buy an apartment she could reasonably furnish, one in which when she calls her kids for dinner, her voice doesn't echo, she likes the space, the anonymity after the thirty years she spent in the ten square blocks around where she grew up, a neighborhood so changed she didn't even want to recognize it anymore. Besides, anyone who rents from her parents these days is as rich as any of her neighbors now. But here, they bring her things: handfuls of basil from their gardens, their children's outgrown bicycles and clothing, and it does not feel as wrong as she imagined it would be to be on that side of kindness.

The girls love the emptiness of the house, the closets with one item in them, the crawl spaces just the right height for their toys, too obvious to hide in and too plentiful not to. It is in one of those spaces that Sunshine convinces Magnolia to hide that afternoon, a game of hide and seek only they know about.

"Now don't move or speak or leave till I come get you." Sunshine secures her sister in the crawl space in a spare bedroom with bags of old stuffed animals, winter blankets, and extra pillows.

"Did you pee?" she asks. It will be hours, the girls predict, before their mom and uncle find Magnolia, before they'll even notice she's gone. A length of time, when told to them, that usually seems interminable, but that now, from their lips, feels like a small victory over the grown-ups.

Magnolia nods, wedging herself against the bags. Sunshine shoves her back with a palm.

"No, in farther, so they can't see you. You can't be wiggling around when they come in. No jumping out when you hear their footsteps either. Got it?"

"Can I have my snacks?"

Sunshine hands over the package of graham crackers in their sleek, oily wax paper.

"Don't eat them all at once. You don't know how long you'll have to be in here."

"Okay."

Magnolia waits till her sister's footsteps reach the bottom of the stairs before she opens her book, which she has squirreled away along with a flashlight, a drawing pad, and a pack of glitter pens on loan from Sunny. She doesn't need to rid her mind of monsters and such; these are the innards of the closets, and she has hidden herself in every dark corner of the house, comfortable as in a womb.

Alison is reentering the yard with two fresh beers when Sunshine jogs past toward the swing set the neighborhood kids share, just beyond a row of hedges.

"Hey, hey, where's your sister?" Alison calls out after her. Magnolia is never but a few leg lengths behind.

"I don't know."

"Could you go get her? I'd like to put the food on soon."

Sunny makes a show of rolling her eyes, but runs back around the front of the house as she's told.

"I can't find her," she announces on her return a few minutes later.

"Well, did you look?"

"Yeah, I looked. I can't find her."

Alison disappears into the shady insides of the house. She calls Magnolia's name as she walks the hallways, making sure her footsteps are audible. She enters every room with a closet, where Magnolia has created small universes of toys—apartments, she calls them—and Alison figures that Sunshine was too lazy to look there. No answer from her younger daughter.

"I can't find her," Alison says when she comes out to the yard again, her hands in the back pockets of her shorts.

"You see?" Sunny says triumphantly, slumped in her mother's patio chair, kicking the air.

Alison ignores her, locks eyes with her brother, asking for his calm. She asks him to go down to the Cramers', the yellow house at the end of the block. "They have these rabbits, and Mag is crazy about them. I'll kill her, though."

Nick almost chuckles at the obviousness of his sister's sending him away, but he's in awe at her ability to put on a lying face when fear must be clawing her insides out. The providence of mothers. "Sure thing."

"I'll go," Sunny volunteers.

"No, you stay here with me. You'll never come back from bunny land." She gathers Sunshine's dirty blond hair into a ponytail around her finger, pulling her toward her, a quick measuring of her body against her own no one else would notice.

She tells Nick to take the yard route while she takes another spin through the house. "And don't pull any of that cop shit over there. It scares people," she yells out after him.

He puts his hand up in the air, a gesture of understanding.


The Cramers' house is the final in a string of connected yards. The grass is still damp from some kid's afternoon run through a sprinkler, mud beginning to return, refreshed, to the earth. Nick sees the rabbits huddled together in a pile in their cage: red wood and wire, a latched door the perfect size for a child's arms to reach in and select a favorite furry friend, something someone's father built. No sign of Mag.

Nick makes himself unassuming (hand in his pocket, a smile that shows his single dimple) as he knocks on the screen door in back—no one in this neighborhood seems to use their front entrances, or lock the ones they do use. He talks briefly with the mother, who invites him in, who expresses alarm and pity just at the mention of his sister and nieces. While he talks with her, her boy, shirtless, the underpinnings of muscle and power in his long and tanned body, on the edge between childhood and puberty, watches him from a stool at the kitchen counter. Nick remembers such boys from his own childhood—the ones who never had to lay a finger on another kid, who ran the neighborhood with their voices or a shift of their eyes. Boys like

Michael, though Nick knows that the likelihood of this kid ending up enthralled by the hustle of New York is slim; he is more likely to be taken in by banking or real estate than petty fraud or apartment burglary.

"Should we call the police?" the mother asks, and Nick assures her there is no need, without telling her what he does.

She promises to send Magnolia back if she spots her. He thanks her and waves good-bye to the boy, who, sitting quietly on his stool, makes no indication that he has seen him at all.

"She'll turn up," the mother says as Nick walks away.

On domestic violence calls or at car accidents, Nick is always handed babies, and they like him, like his smooth, symmetrical face, his wide, firm chest; a child who doesn't know him will stay in his arms as long as he needs it to. He tries, always, to be sweet in front of his nieces, even as they view him with the same indifference as they do most adults—sometimes nice, but all in all disposable. Mag shows him more affection than Sunny, occasionally sitting on his lap or reaching for his hand to hold, only to wiggle out or let go after a couple of minutes, as if she has made a mistake. Sunshine is wary of men altogether; she keeps her distance. Nick remembers when she fell asleep in the backseat of his car on the way home from Thanksgiving last year. He carefully slid his hands under her thighs to carry her into the house, but this only woke her, and her brow crumpled into anger as she moved his hand aside.

"I can go," she said, not pausing to rub her eyes, looking at him hard and unchildlike. He moved out of her way as she got out of the car, slamming her own door behind her.

So when Nick comes around the side of the house to find a young man crouching to inspect Sunny's necklace in the yard, he isn't sure if it's his growing concern about where Mag is that causes the worry about the boy's hands at Sunny's neck, to read into how easily, her chin up, hands on her hips, she is making space for him. Nick waits in the parting of the hedges that leads to the yards beyond his sister's, thinking what best to do, reaching for his logical, alert cop self. The boy is probably a neighbor.

The boy cups the gold charm at the end of the chain in his hand, asking Sunny a question that Nick can't hear clearly. Then a storm passes across his niece's face, a look of betrayal and distrust so intense that Nick wastes no time leaping onto the boy.

Nick pins him in seconds, the boy's thin body not even struggling under the weight of Nick's knees, which he uses to secure the boy to the ground. Sunny stands eye-to-eye with her uncle now, her hands moving to her neck, a red slash of irritation along its right side, where her necklace was a moment ago.

"Scream for your mother," Nick tells her.

Sunny picks up her necklace from the grass, which lies a couple of inches from the boy's contorted face. The necklace once belonged to the great-aunt who owned the house; a medallion with a lion, the astrological sign she shared with Sunny, hung from its center. Her mother kept it stored away till this last birthday, Sunshine's tenth, two weeks earlier.

"Go get her, Sunny. Now."

As her sandaled feet break into a run closer to the house, the boy curses. Nick leans into him and says, "Shut the fuck up."

Nick can tell there is something in his pocket, could be a knife. He puts more pressure on the boy's back, even though he hasn't moved.

"What the hell are you doing?"

"Nothing, man, nothing."

This is the response Nick hears every day. It is rarely the truth.

Alison comes out of the house gripping her daughters' wrists, one in each hand, their skinny arms dangling out of their tank tops. Magnolia was asleep when Alison found her in a closet upstairs. She touched her to wake her, feeling for the warmth of her body, her finger instinctually wiping the bit of drool in the corner of her mouth. The sweat beads at her brow. In the yard, Magnolia's eyes adjust to the light. Sunny is still ashen faced, her summer tan drained. Neither of the girls makes a sound.

"Alison, I have cuffs in my car. In my duffel. In the trunk."

"Do you want your holster?"

She is trying to scare the boy, a tactic she used on Nick in their childhood, that cold, convincing tone—he had always believed she would do anything.

"Just go get the cuffs, please."

Alison pulls the girls back toward the house before dropping their wrists and walking to the car.

"Who knows how to dial 911?" Nick asks the girls.

"I do!" exclaims Magnolia, her round face breaking into a proud smile.

"Mag, go do that for your uncle. Tell them you have an intruder. Answer their questions. Go."

The boy starts to curse again, his protests muffled by the grass. Nick digs his knee into pressure points on the boy's back. Sunny walks from the spot where her mother released her into the thick summer grass and watches the boy twist uselessly on the ground.

"He said he knows my father," she says.

"He's lying," Nick says, although he doesn't know for sure. It wouldn't be unlike one of Michael's friends to show up here, looking for something. Michael took his friends where he could find them.

"He said."

"It's not true."

"How do you know? You don't know my dad."

"Your father's dead," Alison says, handing Nick the cuffs.

"No, he's not." Sunny begins to cry.

"Yes, he is. Go inside," Alison says, a hand, neither soft nor hard, against her daughter's back, turning her toward the house.


The local cops were not pleased to find a teenage boy in handcuffs in the Lymans' backyard. As Nick retold the story to an officer, he could see the youngest cop playing with the girls out of the corner of his eye. It annoyed him, more than it would have if he had just flirted with Alison. There were no charges to press, except on Nick for pouncing on the kid, but the boy, who sat sulking in the back of the squad car in the driveway, declined. Alison didn't recognize him, but the cops did, and while his record of petty theft and the contents of his pockets—more sets of keys than an unemployed nineteen-year-old should reasonably possess—didn't prove anything about his intentions, it was enough to end things there.

Nick restores order in the kitchen, returning the defrosted meat to the fridge, rinsing the beer bottles, while Alison puts the girls to bed. It takes longer than usual to do so. The girls share a room, a habit they will grow out of; one day, she knows, they will use the empty rooms, expand. One day, the house won't be big enough to keep enough space between the three of them.

Sunshine turned to face the wall after Alison read them a few chapters of *The Wonderful Wizard of Oz* from Magnolia's bed, but Magnolia, who talks when she's tired, kept asking questions, even in the dark. *Who was that boy? Why was he here? Can I have more water? Will you get Sunny a new necklace? What will I wear when I die?* She could hear Sunshine, still awake, breathing as Magnolia ran through these questions, but Sunshine, usually the first to tell her sister to shut up, didn't say anything, didn't even mumble when Alison told them to sleep tight, promising to check on Magnolia in ten minutes, by which time she knew the girl would have fallen asleep.

"You're staying?" Alison asks when she comes downstairs to find her brother leaning against the beautiful French doors Aunt Arlene had put in, the ones the girls have covered in fingerprints.

"Sure, I can stay," Nick says, as though he doesn't keep a bag in the trunk for just this reason—a fresh pair of underwear and a shirt, an extra toothbrush.

"That wasn't—" she begins and stops. She reaches to turn the lock on the patio doors, but he's already done it. "The kid's not coming back," she says over her shoulder, moving into the kitchen.

"You bet he's not," Nick says.

"Beer?" she asks him, looking at the neat rows of them in the fridge. "There is certainly enough."

"I'm good," he says, and finally moves from his post at the doors.

She closes the fridge. "I'm going to bed."

"I'll be here."

"I know," she sings as she walks past him on her way upstairs.

"I can go, if you need—"

"No, stay," she says. Her moving to this house was just a matter of geography. *Wherever you go, there you are,* their father likes to say.

As she moves up the stairs, Alison feels in her shorts pocket for the necklace Sunny handed over to her without a word. Fixing it would just be a matter of replacing the chain. She can buy one during her lunch break on Monday, while the girls are in camp. She forgets to check on Magnolia.

Nick sits in the living room on the one couch, in the far corner, with the television tuned to a baseball game he isn't paying any attention to. An hour later, he checks the many doors in the house: the front and the side doors, the garage entrance, the basement, the French doors off the dining room, once more. He needs something stronger than a beer. He leaves his car in the driveway and walks to a neighborhood bar that

Alison took him to last winter, an Irish pub that is loud enough that he can drink at the bar in peace. After a couple of drinks he starts talking to a woman who has been smiling at him from her circle of friends since he sat down. She takes him back to her apartment, a tiny studio that is air-conditioned like a freezer. He leaves before the woman has fallen asleep, although she pretends she has. He nods to the overnight doorman before walking into the summer air, which feels thick and comforting after the cold apartment. The night is quiet, the crickets silent, the streets so empty he walks the final blocks to his sister's house on the yellow lines.

Before Nick can find the right key for the side door in the kitchen, it opens from the other side. "Yo," his sister says.

"Yo," he says back.

She is wearing a T-shirt she's had since high school, her skin visible through the worn shoulders. Her dark hair is in a knot on top of her head. Nick pours himself a glass of water and brings one for Alison, who has sat back down at the banquette by the side door. The time on the oven reads 3:30 A.M.

"I thought you were asleep." He had stood outside her bedroom door before he left for the bar, contemplating telling her he was leaving, but had decided against waking her up.

"I was. Now I'm not." She takes a sip of the water. "Look, can you do me a favor?" she asks as Nick sits down across from her. "Don't tell Mom and Dad, okay?"

"About Michael?"

"About today, the kid."

"I won't."

"Thanks."

The girls will tell her parents about the cops coming by, and Nick will tell them about Michael, another thing he thinks is a favor. She can no more control her brother's overprotectiveness than she could have stopped Michael from choosing the life he did.

"How is Sunny's neck?"

"I put some cream on it. She barely let me touch her; I couldn't get a good look at it."

"Maybe take her in to the doctor on Monday."

"She doesn't like it when we make a big deal out of things like that. She will be fine."

Alison still isn't used to the absolute quiet of the house, the way it settles, the sound of animals skittering across branches outside, acorns bouncing off the roof in fall, how loud a single car can be on a street that's not well trafficked. The refrigerator here is newer than the one in the apartment they lived in just before, and it doesn't hum. It is okay to have her brother there across the table at the hour she usually feels most alone.

"You think he did?" Nick asks her.

She knows immediately that he is talking about the boy from earlier.

"Know Michael?" Alison shakes her head again. "No. God, who did?"

When Nick stood over his former brother-in-law's body hours earlier, he searched for the cool teenager he used to be, the one who, for a few years before Nick knew any better, he wanted to be like. The deformed and bloated mess in a bag was unrecognizable to him.

"That tattoo—"

"The one on his calf?" She had always hated it.

"No, the one on his chest."

She doesn't ask him what it was. She doesn't want to imagine Michael's body anymore.

"Never seen it. Must've gotten it after we split." Alison yawns.

She catches her little brother's eyes fill with tears as he takes a sip of water. When he was eleven, old enough for his looks to interest girls, to take pride in that interest, she had the whole neighborhood calling him Babyface, till she decided, a few years later, he'd had enough. She can still picture the quiver in his lower lip when he got mad at her about it, how he tried and failed to hide his weakness from her. It had always been easy for her to break him. She no longer took pleasure in it. Nor can she take this sadness from him now; there is no act of reversal, no protection against it in her power.

"I don't remember it either," he says, putting his glass back on the table.

In the morgue, Nick focused there, instead of on Michael's busted face, or his lacerated waist, where a knife had gouged over and over. The tattoo was a sunburst above his heart, as if goodness were pouring out from it, or trying to get in.

Upstairs, Sunshine is making her way across the dark room back to her own bed from Magnolia's, which she fell asleep in hours earlier. After their mother had left the room, Mag told Sunny she felt sick. Sunny was so tired, but she didn't want to call their mother back upstairs.

"What's wrong?"

"My stomach."

"Go to the bathroom."

"Okay."

Magnolia pushed off the covers her mother had carefully arranged around her and went.

"Better?" Sunny asked when she came back, suddenly feeling more awake.

"A little."

Sunshine went over to Magnolia's bed without being asked, as they did every so often, a fact they hid from their mother without knowing why. "Scootch," she ordered her sister. She'd stopped whispering by now, their mother so far away in the house she couldn't possibly hear them.

"She's really mad at us," Magnolia said once they'd both settled their heads onto the single pillow.

"We're not in trouble."

The look on their mother's face for the remaining hours of the night, after Mag had been found and the boy had been taken away, was new, she thought, strange, but there hadn't been, and there wouldn't be, any punishment.

"Not yet," Mag insisted.

Sunny knew there was nothing she could say to change her sister's mind, and she didn't want to argue. Mag would feel better in the morning. They'd not play that game again.

# Back Talk

When the boy who barely speaks says to you, *It's too bad, who you are*, into your ear at a party, you know better than to turn your head. You know who he is. It's when he whispers, *Too bad, who you belong to*—this word, *belong*—that your body responds, a shiver he can't detect but that makes you step back toward him. *Because damn*, he says then, *what I wouldn't do to you*. Next he says it dirty, in detail, so quietly no one else knows it's happening. Is it? Do you, after listening, still as a statue while he leans into your ear from behind but doesn't touch you, yet, go with him to a stairway outside the party, slipping out that side door in the kitchen, knowing you'll have to come back for your jacket later, alone? The boy you are dating is his friend. Not his best friend. This boy is dating a freshman on your track team, but you don't hang out with her. Her first boyfriend. Her first heartbreak.

You don't answer him. You don't even look at him, but he

knows to leave his beer behind on the counter, to sit down on the steps a flight up from where the party continues, everyone you know in that packed, parent-free apartment, neither one of you remembering to care. Has it happened? Have you unzipped his pants, plunged your hand in before you've even kissed, your name falling from his mouth like a plea, a spell? In your memory, the stairwell is bright, too bright. And your hand, your mouth around him, a reward for him even speaking to you, for saying what you didn't know you wanted to hear. Your boyfriend doesn't talk either. He doesn't talk about your body or your friends or his friends or his family who you have seen from a distance of fifty feet but never met, the family he is away with right now. Has it happened, you kneeling on the landing, his zipper against your chin, his head thrown back in surprise, how goddamned loud he is all of a sudden, the shock of what he asked for, how much more he received? When you stop, he asks for a tissue.

Has it happened? Of course it has. The boy who does not speak has told everyone by Tuesday. You, though, choose to stay silent: to your boyfriend, to that asshole, to his girlfriend, who believes him, because it's easy to believe what you hear when there is no back talk.

Now, your boyfriend is talking: Was it worth it? Did you like it? Did you think you could get away with it? And you, too, have questions: Was it worth it? Did you like it? Did you think you could get away with it? The questions are for the asshole, the one who, by the time you graduate fifteen months later, single, you realize you've never said a word to. In the stairwell, you just shook your head.

# Lovers' Lookout

Paul arrives on Thursday night and breaks up with Foley on Saturday evening. Afterward, she empties the dinner neither of them had the appetite to eat into the trash. From the kitchen, she listens to him moving in the bedroom they have shared for two years. She brings him a pile of objects to pack with his shirts and jeans: his Cal mug, a frying pan, a set of bookends from his parents' house across the bay. "Please," he says to her as she stands in the doorway, not about their breaking up, but about his things, which he does not want to take cross-country with him. "I'll be back in June," he says. "I can take it then."

He doesn't let her give him anything else to pack in his small suitcase, but in her mind, she removes everything that belongs to him from their apartment, room by room.

The next afternoon, as Foley is tying her running shoes, her mother calls from Saint Louis. When she asks if it's safe for

Foley to run alone in the darkening afternoon, Foley says Paul surprised her for the weekend, that he is going with her. She doesn't tell the truth, how he claimed to have forgotten his running shoes, or how shortly after entering the apartment, he covered the coffee table with piles of his lab reports. How he only paused from his work on them to ask if she has been unfaithful to him, how he was disappointed in her answer that she has not. When Foley talks to her mother, she pretends all his ambitions are still hers, and when her mother asks her to send their love to him, Foley says she will.

Though it has been months since Paul has run with her, she immediately feels the absence of his footsteps alongside hers. They had always been good running partners. He'd insist she pick the route, falling in behind her. She liked the silence on their runs, that he was studying her body, her calves climbing hills, her ponytail sinking to the nape of her neck. Only once they were back at the apartment would he scold her for a burst in her pacing or steep hills. "Trying to lose me again, are you?" he would say, his hands resting on a cramp at his waist.

Afterward they'd share a shower, talking till one of them got cold. It was never Paul, either because he could stand the water longer, or because Foley, relaxed by the run, was the most open with him then. It was in one of those showers that she insisted he take the fellowship in New York, though it meant he'd be gone for nine months. The morning he left she cried, a burst of tears that rose up to her throat as she handed him a cup of coffee for the taxi ride to the airport. Surprised and pleased, he kissed her wet cheekbones and whispered reassurances before bringing his bags downstairs to the waiting car. Last night, when he said,

"I thought if we were apart you might begin to need me more," she didn't know which one of them was the bigger fool.

When Foley reaches the mammoth steps of Buena Vista Park, she is grateful to have made it away from traffic-heavy streets, from the sidewalks littered with couples, their arms looped together. It's a horrible day: overcast, damp, and chilly even before the fog makes its afternoon visit—but perfect for running. There's a cool breeze on Foley's back and no sun to squint at. But the persistent grayness of San Francisco, the fog that swallows bridges and the crests of streets, has ceased to be charming. She misses the seasons she knew growing up, the obvious signs of change.

The hills of the park are filled with wooden planks pushed into the landscape. She takes a series of these steps toward the top of the park, listens to the branches creaking against each other in the wind. Some of the trees are run with thick veins of bark; they shed this skin like snakes onto the path, revealing smooth trunks.

As Foley climbs, the city rises from all sides below her: houses and smaller splotches of green, and soon, water, the ocean and the bay, all from one point. She can see everything she knows from this park, out to Oakland and Marin, the skyline of downtown, the radio tower she uses to orient herself. The layering of fog over distant hills reminds Foley of an O'Keeffe they have in the museum where she works in the education department. When she's with younger kids, the ones who still walk holding each other's hands, she makes them stand before it with their eyes closed for a few giggle-filled seconds, tells them to imagine it as something they'd see out their windows as they are just starting to wake up. As their squinting eyes open, she watches the blurred blue horizon enter their focus.

At the top of the vista point, a man sits on the sole bench, a paperback on his lap. He takes a moment to look up at Foley, a gesture of his harmlessness, and she nods in recognition as she catches her breath.

The man leans forward over his knees, a cigarette between his fingers. "Do you have a light?"

Foley shakes her head, apologizes.

"Of course," he gestures toward her clothes. "You don't smoke."

"No."

"That's good."

Foley turns back to the view. Then, the man asks, quietly, politely, with a hint of an accent she can't yet place, which way the ocean is. She points toward the Pacific. "There, past Golden Gate Park. It's sort of foggy today, so you can't really see . . ." The man is not following her finger, but reading the text on the back of her sweatshirt. It's blue, hooded, from Paul's medical school softball league. He shrank it accidentally, and protested when Foley cut off most of the sleeves so it wouldn't weigh her down. He wanted her to wear it like a cheerleader would wear a boyfriend's letter jacket; she wanted to run in it.

"The Hustler?" the man asks. Paul's nickname, given to him for his enthusiasm for sliding into base, is just discernible under the hood.

"Oh, it's my boyfriend's . . . my . . ." She turns to look at him, noticing the sharp symmetry of his jaw, the tight curl of his hair, a little gray at his temples, his mahogany leather knapsack, from which he has triumphantly dug out some matches. He lays the book on his neatly folded jacket. The book's title is in French. "Where are you visiting from?" she asks as he lights his cigarette.

He says he's in town for a set of interviews at "the university." She doesn't ask which one. "I've never imagined myself in California," he says, "but who knows?"

"Yeah, well, me either," she says.

Six years ago, she moved from Saint Louis to San Francisco to live with a friend; the friend left after four months, but Foley was apprenticing with an artist and stayed. The artist needed her less and less, and she took the museum job a few months later. She met Paul a year after that. As a teenager, when she still believed she would be a painter, she assumed her adult life would be in New York, a city that, when she visited Paul earlier this year, seemed not beautiful enough for her and she not for it, an opportunity that belonged to an earlier version of herself.

"Where are you living now?" she asks him.

"Paris," the man says. "You've been?"

Foley spent her junior year of college at the American university there. There were strikes in the Metro that year, and she walked the city nearly end to end, often missing classes when she'd realize how far she was from where she needed to be. She got to know the streets of Paris rather well, but her mental maps of the city are faded now. Still, she asks him where, and they begin to talk about how he taught architecture and history at the same school she studied at, about how much he likes teaching American students, their curiosity. He's ready for a change, he tells her.

Foley is sitting down on the wall by the man's feet when the weather really worsens, a low sweeping of clouds and fog they can see moving toward them. Her runner's body is no use against the wind. Goose bumps rise on her shins; her sweat feels cold underneath her armpits.

When the man asks her to grab a cup of coffee, it seems entirely logical, a way to keep talking and get warm. She has tried to forget how lonely these past five months have felt while Paul has been in New York.

Foley looks down at her running shoes. She says she doesn't have any money on her, and he laughs, jingling some change in his pocket. The gesture is both crude and inviting, and she likes the way his face lights up as he does this.

He has lit a second cigarette in the time they have been talking. She reaches out in an offer to hold it while he gathers his things. Foley has never been a smoker herself, but she grips his cigarette between her fingers as if it's her own. She flicks an ash, remembering a boyfriend in college she used to do this for while he closed his coat or put on a hat. When she hands the cigarette back to the man, she tells him her name, and he tells her his before putting the cigarette back in his mouth. Stefan.

They take the shorter paths through the trees. She walks ahead of him, but he keeps up with her on the unevenly spaced steps, even in his wingtips. When they reach the larger paved walkways, Foley points out the headstones used to make the park's gutters, thinking it is the type of thing, like her knowledge of the jazz clubs in the 19th arrondissement, that will impress him.

"Here, look," she says, crouching down to push back the dead leaves and tree skins, showing him the pieces of marble with numbers and letters still visible. Paul taught her these facts she's now telling Stefan, that the stones are leftovers of unclaimed graves from when the city moved the cemeteries to Daly City. Paul learned it as a teenager, volunteering for the parks service. Nearly every place she knows in the city is a spot from Paul's youth, or a place they discovered together. She understands why the living wouldn't want to sleep near the dead.

Stefan bends at his knees to run his fingertips over the etchings in the marble. The slabs, cut into neat octagons, are laid in tight like puzzle pieces. His head close to hers, he smells only faintly of nicotine, and mostly of a kind of musk, a hair product or an aftershave. "The French did that, long ago, pushed the bodies outside the city walls. You know, like Père Lachaise, where Morrison is," Stefan says as he straightens up. He uses a blue lighter from the inside pocket of his jacket to start another cigarette.

Foley leads Stefan the few blocks to the Hungry Dog, a café where she and Paul often had brunch. They are offered a seat by the window, but remembering Paul's friends who share an apartment around the corner, she asks for a table closer to the bar. "Warmer back there," she explains.

Stefan motions for her to sit before he does. She doesn't recognize the waitress, who smells of a peachy perfume, the kind that makes Foley think of teenagers, though this woman is about her own age. Stefan says he thinks he has been here before, with the friend whose apartment he is staying at, friends of his brother who are in France for a while. The street he's told her it's on is higher even than the lookout at Buena Vista. They talk about these friends, the neighborhood, about the job Stefan is considering, about his American mother and Moroccan father. Foley tells him about the collections at the museum, about how, on stressful days, she wishes she could run home from work rather than be packed against everyone else on the Muni. She misses walking Paris.

"You and your boyfriend live close by?"

"Fiancé," she says, the lie falling from her mouth as easily as the one she told her mother earlier. This, too, was a possible version of events: There had been a ring in Paul's suitcase last summer on a visit they made to Saint Louis. She saw the unmistakable outline of the box between his summer-weight shirts when she was looking for his dopp kit so she could borrow a razor. She slid her fingers between the shirts and rubbed the velvet cover but didn't open it. They were in town for a high school friend's wedding. That night at the reception she drank too much, flirted with the boys she'd grown up with, who had become men she still wasn't interested in. When she dropped her drink at the edge of the dance floor, its thick glass bouncing off the reception hall's carpet, Paul crouched down with her to retrieve it, a napkin already in his hand to wipe their shoes, and suggested quietly that she skip a refill. She told him to relax as she stood back up, her fingers sticky with tonic.

"Just thinking about how you're going to feel in the morning," he said, slipping an arm around her waist.

"You don't have to be the fucking doctor all the time," she

said before walking to the bar on the other side of the floor. Paul stood with the wet napkin next to an old friend of hers she'd led him to believe was an ex, when she'd only kissed him once or twice, a scrambling of hormones and boredom. "Are you still doing that art thing?" the fake ex had asked her at the cocktail hour earlier. Paul had never even seen one of her paintings; she'd left them in her parents' attic in Saint Louis, assured she'd come back for them once she settled into a place she could paint in. "Foley is going to run the SFMOMA one day," Paul had said, and Foley changed the subject. She spent the rest of the night moving out of whatever circle of her old friends Paul was standing in.

She knew her behavior toward Paul was cruel and juvenile, but after three days of her family fawning over his accomplishments and California good looks, after seeing that ring that he was so sure he could convince her she wanted, though they'd never even discussed the possibility, she had felt relieved to put this distance between them, even if only for the night.

By the time they boarded the plane back to California, she had apologized to him, joking that now they'd be banned from the Saint Louis wedding circuit forever and that he was very welcome.

"I liked it," he said, lifting the shade on Foley's window seat. "I like where you're from."

Her head already throbbing, Foley found her sunglasses in her bag and put them on without a word to Paul. He left for New York the following month. She wonders now, in the café, whatever happened to the ring, if it's in her apartment somewhere, still in its velvet box.

The busboy brings them water in glasses that are still warm from the dishwasher. Foley puts her hands to the heat of hers.

When the coffee arrives shortly after, Foley thanks Stefan. "My pleasure," he says. Then, after a few sips, he says, "I thought American girls liked big diamond rings," indicating her bare hands.

"It slipped once, so I don't run with it on," she lies. "And you?" she asks. "Married?"

Stefan holds up his left hand, which she already knows is without a ring. "I also leave my diamonds at home." She laughs, which pleases him. "No, not anymore," he says. "Once. We are still good friends. She remarried. But it's not for me," he says, waving the idea of marriage away like it's a plate he's finished with. He shifts the canister of sugar to the side of the table. "But maybe it's for you—for you and . . . ?"

"Paul."

"For you and Paul."

"Maybe."

"You're young; you will see."

"I'm twenty-eight."

"Young," he repeats, smiling.

She thinks of her cousins, years younger, who have houses and babies, to whom she seems old, or at least foolishly slow.

"And he doesn't mind, your fiancé, you having coffee with me?"

"He's in New York."

She tells him about Paul's research fellowship, how competitive the program is, about his work on early-onset dementia.

"Sounds like a smart young man."

"He is."

"You don't worry about him, in New York? All those beautiful women."

"He's not the cheating type."

Stefan shrugs. "Everyone is the cheating type, don't you think? When presented with the right opportunity?"

"Maybe," she says. It hasn't occurred to her, what motivated Paul's question about her faithfulness.

"Is that what happened," she asks, "with your ex?"

Stefan shakes his head. "No, nothing so dramatic."

"You just weren't right for each other?"

He waves this away, too. "The only place a man and a woman are right for each other is in bed. And that has nothing to do with anything else."

Foley thinks back to sex with Paul this weekend, recalling the force with which he entered her just yesterday morning; she thought his uncharacteristic fumbling was a product of jet lag and pent-up desire, but their compatibility in bed was likely the last item on the list he'd been desperate to check off. Paul had always been systematic, a planner.

"I mean, think of the best sex you've ever had. Not your fiancé, right?" Stefan asks.

"A Frenchman, actually." Henri was Belgian, really, a friend of a friend on her study abroad year in college. "In Paris."

"And what was so great about it? Were you in love?"

Foley laughs, though she doesn't mean to. "No, we were most definitely not." Henri had a girlfriend, a beautiful German girl she didn't like very much, an excellent painter who was enrolled in the same studio art program as Foley. She doesn't know if he ever told her, and while Foley liked to imagine the girlfriend's coldness to her in their shared studio all year was because of Henri, it was, she thinks, because Foley was a far inferior painter, not as serious as Claudine, not as committed to her art.

"He belonged to someone else," she tells Stefan. "It felt won."

"Ah," he says. "That."

Foley notices a slight tremor in her hands. It's the coffee, she tells herself, hitting her system all at once. She tries to remember what she has eaten since this morning. Half an apple after she made a pile of Paul's books on the bedroom floor; later, cold noodles over the sink, throwing the pieces of shrimp into the trash can. She excuses herself, hoping she appears steady as she walks past Stefan toward the restrooms in the back.

In the tiny bathroom, she assesses herself in the mirror. Her face is flushed from the run and the cold—healthy, her grandfather would say. She cannot do anything about her running clothes, about the way she is sure she has the faint smell of sweat on her, but she can do something about her hair, which she has been growing long since Paul left for New York. She undoes her ponytail, combing her hair with her fingers, putting the elastic in the trash can. She takes a squirt of hand lotion by the sink to smooth back the wild hairs, a trick a friend taught her. She recognizes the peachy scent of the waitress. She removes Paul's sweatshirt. Underneath, she wears a slim-fitting running top that shows what few curves a sports bra offers. She puts lotion on the cracked skin of her hands, on her chest, where she lowers the zipper of her running shirt.

When she returns to the table, Stefan is laughing with the same waitress, his lips curled invitingly. Foley tucks her hair behind her ear as she sits down again, giving the waitress her own smile, one that sends her back to the coffee station with the now-empty pot.

"You came back," he says.

"Well, the back fence is very high. Even in these shoes."

"I'm glad for that."

"I'm glad, too."

"And you're warmed up," he says. She's hung the sweatshirt by its hood on the back of her chair.

"Yes, thank you. The coffee helps."

Her cup has also been refilled by the waitress, and although she does not think she can stomach any more, Foley pours in the milk and stirs her sugar while Stefan watches her.

"Tell me something," he says, leaning in, his palms flat on the table.

"About what?"

"Anything: music, books, where you like to walk in the city, where you like to eat. Tell me why I should stay."

She used to like these conversations with men who wanted to know so much about her; she used to like to figure out how much to give them and what, exactly, would keep them asking for more. But today, she just feels tired.

"You first."

He takes her hand across the tabletop, lacing his fingers with hers. She hoped that when they first touched it would be more urgent—a two-handed grab of her waist—but the way he reaches for her is gentle, nearly clumsy. "Okay. This one," he says, tugging on her empty ring finger, "is connected to your heart. Goes right to it. Not your brain, but your heart."

"Who told you that, a fortune-teller?"

"My ex-wife, actually." As suddenly as he first took them, he's let go of her fingers, and as immediately, she wants to stay in his hands, to be touched again.

"Same difference then, yes?"

He lifts up his hands in a gesture of defeat.

"Look, I loved my ex-wife, very much. Some others as well, of course. But you know how it is—with Paul. You're in love; it's special; it's very, very beautiful, for however long it lasts."

"So you're an optimist."

"Marriage was not for me and Joelle, not then. But love is something else. And sex, well . . . But you are young, and smart, and very beautiful," he says, "and you will be fine. Do not listen to a bitter unemployed Frenchman."

When Foley looks out the restaurant's windows, she can see the streetlights have come on. It will be a cold walk home; she is too wired on the wrong kinds of energy to run. The dinner crowd has started to come in, couples meeting for the first time or the tenth at the restaurant bar, husbands and wives and partners who've said yes to one another for a night or a year or decades, who keep saying yes in a way she doesn't know how. She imagines that they are happy, but who can say? Aren't they imagining the same about her and Stefan, justifying the fifteen-year age gap between them, finding charm in the contrast of his neatly rolled shirtsleeves and expensive jacket with her faded running clothes? Did it seem to everyone else that when he held her hand in his a minute ago, he was affirming their intertwined purpose, that he was delivering her a promise? Could anyone tell that they've spent the past three hours feeding each other lies?

"Why me?" Foley asks.

"Why you what?"

"Why, in the park today, did you pick me?"

"Is that what happened? I picked you?"

Foley remembers the last time she ran through that section of the park, up where the bench is at the vista point. She had taken a day off from work for a doctor's appointment. She went on an early afternoon run. There was a couple on that bench at the top, their bodies pressed against each other, the man's hands roving up the woman's skirt, oblivious to hikers and dog walkers. Foley ran past them twice, her feet snapping twigs, and still, they did not separate. It was a lovers' lookout. Of all the things she had found while running through that park—empty bottles of prescription pills, pine cones covered in moss, clusters of banana slugs, abandoned job applications for coffee shops— this had been the most startling, the white skin of the woman's thigh, and the peek of her panties that Foley could not help but see. Not the remnants of people's lives she could imagine happening before and after, but the real thing.

"The lighter," she says.

"You're a smart girl. You played along."

"And why did I seem like the kind of woman you could take home?"

"Are you coming home with me?"

"Isn't that what you want?"

"Of course," he says, "if that's what you want." The waitress brings the check and lays it in the middle of the table. Neither of them thanks her. Despite everything she's had to drink, Foley's throat feels dry. "My flat is just a few blocks from here," he says.

"No," she says. "Why don't we meet tomorrow, in the park, at the vista point? Is seven thirty too early?"

"I don't want to go for a run."

"Me neither." Foley gets up from her chair, folding her sweatshirt over her arm. She kisses Stefan on both cheeks and walks out of the restaurant, leaving him to pay the bill.

In the morning, Foley showers and dresses for work. She wears a soft wool skirt, short boots with a flat sole so she can climb the park steps with ease. She's been thinking about it since she left Stefan last night. She won't bother taking off her boots. She wants him to touch her hair, clean and dry, to lift it off her neck with his strong hands. In her ear, he can tell her all the lies he wants, or he can say nothing at all. With Paul, it had been a routine down to when the lights were switched off, tip to toe each piece of clothing a negotiation, as though there was any question how it would end. She and Stefan will lie down on one of their jackets or he will back her up against a fallen tree, and it will be fast, and it will be done. She hasn't decided if she will ask to see him again.

It's foggy again in the park. She's on time. She waits, on her feet, for ten minutes, half an hour. She has a stack of grants to edit in her work bag, but that's not what she wants to be doing when Stefan comes. Forty minutes, and a man with three off-leash dogs, around him in a loose circle of togetherness, approaches. He says hello to her. He's young and handsome and too scruffy to be her type and she smiles at him and as he smiles back she realizes she is the romantic one, and she is the brutal one. Paul was one of those and Stefan is neither. She misread his desire as indecency.

As she descends the hill toward the bus to work, the same bus on which she had seen Paul four years ago, folding his newspaper into perfect columns, and decided to lay claim to him, she remembers another thing he taught her about Buena Vista Park. During the 1906 earthquake, residents climbed to the top of the park to watch the city burn. For five days the fires spread out before them, and their old city would have to become new again. Foley secures the snaps on her work bag and begins to run, not at a jogger's pace, but at a wild, inconsistent sprint.

# Dinosaurs

On Friday night, babysitting night, Claire waited at the end of the driveway, her breath appearing in the air before her. She pulled her wool hat over her damp hair and crossed her arms and watched for the gunmetal gray of Noah Hunt's sports car to appear around the corner of Trellen Street. Claire didn't care for cars, but she loved sinking into the low seat of this one, the feel of its cold leather against her back, the hum of talk radio, the smooth stops and starts. Noah, as he had always insisted she call him, lifted his fingers from the steering wheel in a wave as he pulled up.

Noah smelled like shampoo and toothpaste and wool. Claire noted the freshly pressed pants, the cashmere sweater—not the blue jeans of poker nights or the college sweatshirt of a movie alone. A date, Claire decided as she clicked her seatbelt into place and said hello. If her own father or brother had seemed that hopeful, she would have told him how handsome he looked. But as his kids' babysitter she could only say, "Thanks for coming to get me."

"Of course. This wind has been out of control, huh?" The wind had been snatching the leaves from the trees all week.

Half a year from a driver's license, Claire walked over to the house most nights, but Noah picked her up when the weather turned cold or wet. It was the least he could do, he said, since he could never take her home at the end of the night.

Claire's mother, who worked in Noah's office, told her how his wife had died: a brain aneurysm at their local swimming pool two and a half years earlier. Lauren Hunt had slid into the water from the edge of the pool, her book tumbling gently from her hands, as if she were falling asleep under the late August sun. The children, who had been floating in front of her in water wings, were now five and seven.

As Noah's hands turned the leather-covered steering wheel, Claire noticed that the tan line from his wedding band was only now, at the onset of winter, beginning to blend in with his skin. She wondered when he'd decided to take the ring off, if he woke up confused some mornings—the way she did in hotel rooms on vacation, or at sleepovers, in the temporary strangeness of the bed—if he still reached for his wife across the mattress.

When Claire and Noah entered the house, Hadley and Thomas were in their pajamas at the kitchen table, bowls of spaghetti positioned between their elbows. Their hair was clean and damp, their feet in slippers, their glasses full of milk. Their aunt Elizabeth, already changed into her scrubs for the evening's shift at the hospital, was finishing the last of the dishes.

Thomas sucked in a noodle with a loud slurp.

"Claire's here!" Hadley announced.

The dog, Mickey, danced at Claire's legs, offering her his backside to scratch.

"Well, my presence is clearly not needed anymore." Elizabeth smiled at Claire, drying her hands on a dish towel. "I'm off, monkeys," she said, and kissed her niece's and nephew's cheeks.

As she pulled on her coat at the kitchen door, Elizabeth poked Noah's chest. "You have some fun tonight, will you?"

"I will certainly try," he said. When he caught Claire's eye, he gave her an embarrassed grin before telling her he was going to get an umbrella. So it was a date.

Claire twirled the ends of Hadley's hair as she took the seat between the kids at the table. Thomas, the little one, reached out to pat her hand.

"Hello," he said, his mouth full of pasta.

"Hello," she said back.

When Claire began sitting for the kids a year earlier, Thomas had climbed into her arms within minutes of the sound of the garage door closing after Noah's car. He wrapped his arms and legs around her with the force of a python, put his head on her shoulder, and released a breath.

"Oh," she had said, to no one in particular.

"He does that with girls. It's because he misses Mommy," Hadley explained, her head cocked in a practiced sympathy.

"Okay," Claire said, and almost cried under the weight of Thomas's grip.

Noah pulled out of the driveway slowly, waiting for the kids to appear at the picture window as they always did when he left for the night. Claire's arms were wrapped around Hadley's shoulders. Thomas grinned, waving with both hands. Noah liked Claire. She wasn't precocious or flirtatious, as so many other of the babysitters had been, even when—especially when—Lauren was still alive. Claire didn't ask too many questions; the kids loved her. There had been two babysitters before, both older women, whom he couldn't keep, who had asked too much about Lauren, about his personal life.

In the year after Lauren's death, his friends and family treated him with varying degrees of pity and disapproval, some offering to set him up on dates, others constantly dragging up memories of her—there were nine calls on her birthday. Hadley's teachers called him in for "check-ins" nearly every month, though there wasn't any real progress to report, just repeated suggestions that he seek more support. Acquaintances stopped him at the market, pulled him aside at soccer games, said, *She should be here*, and *I still can't believe it*. His face would turn into a sad mirror of theirs, and he would nod, even though it was impossible for him not to believe it: Lauren's death had been instantly real; she wasn't there anymore.

In late spring, he put the house on the market, just to see. When Lauren's brother drove by the FOR SALE sign on their front lawn, he parked his car across the street and called Noah, asked him to consider the stability of the kids, to think of Lauren's parents, who lived just a few miles away. But as much as they had been there for him and the kids in the months following Lauren's death, Noah needed space from them, too. The house sold within weeks, and Noah took this as a sign that they should go. Elizabeth helped him find a new house close to hers, in a suburb much like the one they were moving from, just in the other direction, outside the city. He drove to the new town on the last day in June, the dog in the front seat, Hadley and Thomas in the back, suitcases in the trunk, the moving truck a few hours ahead of them.

Noah thought of how deceptively simple it had been to inhabit their new life. The kids liked their schools; they found a new favorite ice-cream shop and playground by the end of that first summer. Noah had given away most of Lauren's personal things, and settling into the new house without them had given him the first feeling of lightness and relief he'd had since her death. He had that feeling now, of possible and inevitable forward motion, as he merged onto the highway toward the first date he'd agreed to in two years. If this dinner was a date; he wasn't sure. *I'm so excited to see you*, Sarah had said on the message she'd left on his voice mail. Sarah was in town on business; Noah hadn't seen her since college. They had belonged to the same loose circle of friends through which he'd met Lauren his junior year, and the three of them would study together sometimes. Then, he was distracted by trying to win Lauren's affection; she'd told him she didn't want to date anyone at their small school, that she'd had enough awkward exchanges with exes on campus already. Sarah was even more out of reach;

she had perfect glassine skin and soft black curls, and spent her summers as a fitness model. Noah had waited for her face to spring up in one of those health magazines Lauren used to read, but it never did. It was only now, driving to meet Sarah, that he realized that he'd had a crush on her, too—minor and forgettable, but a crush. Her voice, low and self-assured, rang in his head on the drive into Boston.

When she could hear the deep breathing of sleep from their rooms, not the fake snoring Hadley always tried at first, Claire called her boyfriend, Eli. She held the phone to her ear while he talked about the next morning's swim meet, the first of his senior season. *Kelsey said there are supposed to be scouts there.* Claire walked the house as she listened—through the kitchen, the living room in circles. *I just wish it wasn't the first one.* She checked her teeth in a bathroom mirror, opened the cabinet with the cookies, the drawer with the beer. *I had that dream last night, where I'm on the block in a snowsuit.* She sat at the bottom of the steps, rubbed her fingers over the nap of the carpet. *My left shoulder's been popping a little in practice, but I think it's okay.* She leaned on the doorway of Noah's room; the smell of his shower still clung to the wallpaper. *You'll be there, right?* Claire considered going in; she'd never been in his room before. *Claire?* She flicked on the light in the bedroom, one arm stretched across the doorway. *You still with me?*

"I should go. My battery is dying."

Noah's room was impeccable. There was only one nightstand, a book on it, a lamp, an alarm clock. A picture of Hadley and Thomas sat on the dresser. She realized it was the only room where there wasn't a picture of Lauren.

"Can you call on the house phone, then?" Eli asked.

Claire walked to the bed and sat down. She wondered if Noah kept to one side or if he drifted to the middle, got tangled in the blankets. Did he let Hadley and Thomas climb in during the night, use them to fill the space of Lauren's body? Claire thought of her own parents' bedroom, of her father's reading glasses on the bedside table, of her mother's knitting in a heap on the floor, of their nightly rituals, silent and synchronized.

"My ear hurts," she said, rising to turn off the light. Claire retreated, hoping her feet hadn't made small impressions in the carpet. "I'll see you at eleven."

Eli couldn't sleep on nights before meets or games, and he had offered to pick her up. Noah always minded the time, and although they had a system for him being late—he was to call Claire's cell phone—he never used it, never took a minute longer than he had promised to.

"At eleven, then."

"See you soon."

"I'll miss you."

Claire laughed softly. "See you soon," she repeated.


Noah met Sarah at the restaurant; she rose from her seat and gathered him in a tight hug. When they separated, he could see that she was more beautiful than she had been in college; girl-ishness had never suited her. She wore a sweater that dipped beneath her collarbones, accentuating her long neck; she kept a hand on its milky length throughout most of dinner, her other hand lifting her wineglass, jeweled rings sparkling under the warm yellow lights.

"It's so good to see you," she said, lingering on the word *so*. Noah wondered if it was a pause of attraction or pity. "You too," he said.

They had married in the same year, sent regrets for each other's weddings, but after that their correspondence had faded the way most acquaintances' did; it had been over ten years since they'd spoken. When Lauren died, Sarah wrote him a note, filling both flaps of the card with the loopy script he hadn't seen since their chemistry flash cards: *I remember that you two were beautiful together, that Lauren radiated happiness when she was around you.* The note came in with the flood of others from people who had rediscovered his address when they'd heard the news. He remembered hearing through the same network of friends about Sarah's marriage ending within a few years, about her move to California soon after. He also remembered how Lauren, when he passed the news of Sarah's divorce on at dinner one night, had remarked on how Sarah had always been drawn to the wrong men. "Sad, but not a surprise," she had concluded with a shrug.

Sarah put her elbows on the table, her hands clasped under her chin. "Who would've thought we'd be having dinner like this?"

"It's been a long time," Noah said, shifting the napkin on the table with his fingertips.

"When I knew I'd be nearby, I had to call and see how you were."

Noah and Lauren had always lived close to Boston, but

Sarah had never felt compelled to call before. "Do you come here often?" he asked.

At this, Sarah's face erupted into a magazine-worthy smile, and then a laugh she couldn't keep in, playful and sweet. Noah shook his head, embarrassed, but laughing, too. "I meant to Boston, for business, not—"

"I'm a Libra, if that's your next question," she teased him.

Without the safety of their previous arrangements—in college, Lauren had in the end waited for Noah after their study dates—Noah realized that Sarah, too, had carried something for him, something small and throwaway that now could be real. That Lauren's death had allowed for this filled him with anger and longing.

By the time the waiter came over with their appetizers, their conversation was easy, flirtatious even. Like the dates he would have gone on, Noah thought, had he dated after college rather than marrying his wife.

But at a mention of a school project Noah had been helping Hadley with, Sarah released her spoon into her soup and put her hand over her mouth.

"I'm sorry," she said, taking in air sharply.

"It's okay," he said back, as he always did.

Sarah's voice dropped to a whisper, like his daughter's did when she was upset. "I just remember her talking about that name—it was her mother's?"

"Her grandmother's maiden name." Noah was reminded that Sarah and Lauren had really been friends, that it was this fact that had kept his crush from being real, a fact he had been trying to forget.

Sarah put her napkin to her damp, beautiful eyes and Noah patted the hand that still lay on the table, the way he had learned to do after the funeral. How easily he gathered others' hands in his own now, channeling grief through his skin, relieving others of their sorrow for his loss. The idea was wondrous to him; there was no section of his brain in which Lauren lived that he could just give away. Noah had been collecting other people's feelings for Lauren—their truths and confessions and tiny memories—for more than two years now, and imagined he would for the rest of his life.

Sarah's fingers didn't curl up around Noah's as he had hoped they would, his touch perhaps too sincere, too hungry. She apologized again as she extracted her hand from under his, excusing herself to the restroom. No waiters came by to fill his water, or the mostly full wineglasses, and Noah sat alone, no longer hungry, over his salad plate. When Sarah came back from the restroom, her smile was timid and ashamed, and while he tried again to make a quick joke, to make her laugh the way he had before, the best he could coax from her was a few weak nods. Through the rest of their meal, they talked of other things, of the people they had known in college, halfheartedly traded gossip that was not about either of them.

It had started to rain during dinner: big, cold drops that landed forcefully on the sidewalk. Noah walked Sarah back to her hotel, holding an umbrella over both of them, minding the fraught space between their bodies. They hugged again in the lobby, and he told her to call the next time she was in town, but she made no promises, only told him that it had been nice to catch up and wished him a safe drive back. His car smelled faintly of coffee and the graham crackers Thomas had recently crushed under his thighs in the backseat, and of the rain soaking into his wool coat. Noah turned onto the highway toward home.

Claire was sitting on the couch with a magazine when Noah returned at 10:40. As usual, he paid her more than he should have and asked if she had a way home. He knew that sometimes Claire lied and said someone was coming, but she only pretended to wait and would walk home by herself. The town was certainly safe enough, and he couldn't have gotten her home himself anyway, but he wanted to acknowledge that he understood she was trying to do him a favor. It was one of the things he liked about her, that even her lies were considerate.

"My boyfriend is on his way." She looked at her phone for the time. "I should wait outside."

"I'll wait with you," he said. "I've got to let the dog out anyway."

They sat on the front steps, the concrete cold through Claire's jeans. Mickey rustled the bushes along the fence, hunting for a tennis ball.

"Your boyfriend a nice guy?" Noah knew he was breaking a rule by asking this, but it felt good, normal, to ask after someone else.

"I'm thinking of breaking up with him but yes, he's nice."

"I'm sorry."

Claire shook her head. "Don't be."

When Eli had said he loved her, the best she could muster

was an apologetic look that sent his feelings back to him as unacceptable, as though they were a too-rare piece of meat.

The dog dropped the ball at Noah's feet. He pitched it across the front lawn.

"How was your date?" she asked him.

Noah shrugged. "It was okay."

The hopefulness Claire had sensed before was gone. "It was awful," she said.

"Yes, it was awful," he said, and laughed. "Not much better than high school dating, apparently."

Claire laughed back, and slid off her wool hat, held it in her hands. It wasn't so cold out; the night had calmed the wind, and the rain that was coming their way made the air thick. For her hair alone, copper red and shiny, as though it would be hot to the touch, Claire knew men looked at her: college students in restaurants downtown, fathers at high school football games. When she began to understand what it was they were looking at her for, she had taken to tucking her hair under a baseball cap, and she thought about cutting it short, but she loved it too much herself. She liked the feel of a boy running his fingers all the way down its length, and sometimes even knowing that by taking the cap off, she was getting them to see her, just at the moment she wanted to be seen.

Noah didn't look at her then, but Claire thought he never really looked at anyone, and especially not at women.

"Maybe you aren't ready yet," she said to him.

"Maybe not," he said, crossing his arms over his knees. "But I'm lonely, I guess."

Claire thought she understood. How strange, how sudden Noah's loneliness must have been. It was different from the way Thomas was lonely—primitive and confusing, occupying the shadow of his every look at the world. And it was different from the way Eli, despite everyone loving him—because of it—was lonely. Noah's loneliness didn't seem to want to be fixed, not now, anyway.

Claire could see Eli's car idling at the gate. "That's him," she said, rising from the step and sliding her bag onto her shoulder.

Noah wished he could get a look at the boy whose heart he was sure Claire would break. "Good luck," he said as she walked down the path from the steps. She gave Mickey's ears a quick scratch before she closed the gate behind her.

Eli didn't take her straight home. He drove around the neighborhood slowly, the stereo on low. Claire looked at the passing houses, the cars tucked neatly into the driveways. Eli turned off the headlights at the dead end at Indian Pond. They didn't unbuckle their seatbelts; they didn't touch. Their conversation steamed the car windows.

Eli had been her boyfriend since spring. He was quiet and smart and athletic, the kind of boy the mothers called lovely. Claire thought her own mother wanted the relationship to work more than she did herself, always inviting Eli over for family dinners and showing up at his football games. The sex, too. Her mother had asked Claire if she needed birth control, and when she said she wasn't sleeping with Eli, her mother had said, *Why not?* and then apologized, laughing a little. *You just let me know when you need it.* Claire sensed that her mother wanted all the ugliness of her daughter's growing up over with, as though the pain she was sure to experience was best to happen quickly. Claire wanted these years before adulthood, ugly as they might be, to take their time. She wanted her mother to be wrong.

"You've been quiet," Eli said.

"I've been listening."

They both sat facing the windshield.

"You do that a lot."

"What's that mean?"

"I saw you sitting outside with him, with that babysitter guy."

"So?"

"You doing something with him?"

"Eli."

"Claire?"

She looked at him, his hands resting on the wheel as if he were still driving. She thought about how Eli wouldn't be able to sleep that night, how on top of the scouts, he would worry about her, and she would worry, too, because he needed to sleep. She thought that when he came to his senses, he would see that swimming was a surer bet than she was.

Claire felt unbearably warm in the car. She put her hand on the door.

"I'm going to walk home, okay?"

"Claire, what is going on?"

"I need to walk."

She unbuckled her seatbelt, leaned across the gearshift to touch the soft fuzz at his hairline; he'd just cut his hair short for the season. She took his face in her hands and turned it toward her. She could feel his heart beating through her fingertips, fast and clear, the way he tells her it does on the starting block, the way it must reverberate in his ears when he pushes through the water. She loved this pulse, its constancy, its predictability.

"Let me drive you."

Claire shook her head, kissed his perfect nose before she pushed the door open. "I just need to walk. Everything is okay. Sleep tight."

She heard the window rolling down as she walked away. "You'll be there tomorrow, right?" he called out after her.

Claire wanted to be there for him in the morning, to be wrapped in that warm bleached air of the school pool, everything turquoise and slippery. But she didn't promise him anything as she pulled her hat over her hair and headed down the road.

Noah was turning off the outside light when he saw Claire across the street. She stepped forward off the curb; the street-light caught her hair like a match being lit. She worried the tight loops of her hat between her fingers. "You okay?" he asked her from the front step, his voice at regular volume, the street so quiet his question carried to her.

Claire crossed the road without checking for cars. "Fine."

Noah walked out into his dark front yard, meeting her at the gate. She looked to him for permission before unlatching it; he nodded and pushed it open for her. That afternoon, while Noah had gathered fallen leaves into bags, Thomas had planted his rubber dinosaurs in the grass; they stretched across one side of the yard in a neat zigzag pattern. Claire stepped between them delicately and deliberately, as though she had put them there herself.

"I didn't do it. I didn't break up with him," she told him. "Maybe my mother is right. Maybe I should just sleep with him. Get it over with."

Noah pictured Claire's mother, square jawed and serious, her tight New England smile as she sat across her desk from a client. He could hardly imagine her suggesting this to her soft, sensitive daughter.

"You shouldn't do that." He looked Claire in the eye as he said this.

Claire nudged a dinosaur with the toe of her sneaker till it fell over.

Noah's legs felt heavy. He sank into the brittle grass of the yard, the leaves that had already fallen since he'd raked breaking underneath his back as he lay down. He closed his eyes. He could hear Mickey whapping his tail against the storm door, wanting out. He let him whine.

The sudden weight of Claire's skull over his heartbeat felt wrong, the way it had felt wrong to want so badly to see Sarah tonight, or to come home to a house with a kitchen on the left of the door rather than the right, or how Thomas looked less like his wife as he got older, the way everything had felt wrong, underneath the impression of being right. He stroked Claire's long, beautiful hair as though it were his daughter's, or his dead wife's, or Sarah's, and it was just another Friday night. He remembered one, or maybe it was a dream he kept having, he wasn't sure, but it was Friday night, and he was in bed with his wife, and there weren't any kids yet, and she was teasing him about a teenage girl at the movie theater, how she'd blushed as he passed by. He'd pinched his then-new wife, playfully, and he did it again in the yard to Claire, on the back of her arm, to see if she felt anything, to see if she might pinch him back.

# Gone

Mirabelle and I began collecting the names of the dead girls in December, after Marissa Hull fell out of an apartment window on Broadway. Marissa, fifteen, was six months pregnant, and although she was alone in the apartment before she died, there was little to suggest you could fall out a fourteenth-floor window in December, backward, without trying. Her sister, Helen, was in homeroom down the hall from us. We didn't go to Marissa's funeral, or the funerals of the other dead girls—forty-three by the next September.

We used the notebook Mirabelle's mother had given her as an early Christmas present; Mrs. Diehl had hoped Mirabelle would work out some of the adolescent moodiness that had hit her harder than the rest of us that year. "Fuck that," she told me Christmas night, tossing the notebook to me across my bedroom. The brown leather book, bound with suede ties, thudded next to me on my unmade bed.

"Merry Christmas," she added.

Our parents were downstairs, finishing off the wine Mirabelle's parents had brought for Christmas dinner. Their laughter came up to us through the radiators, tinny and ghostlike.

"It's nice. You sure you don't want it?" Mirabelle and I had always traded a small present or two, but I thought Mrs. Diehl would be upset if she knew Mirabelle had so eagerly given away this gift. When I opened the journal, Marissa Hull's name was in the top left corner of the first page. "Oh, you can just cross that out." Mirabelle waved her hands, brushing the name away. She pulled on the new purple-and-yellow-striped gloves my mother had knitted for her.

Then Mirabelle explained she'd been having dreams—in them, she'd be standing in front of the dry cleaner's across the street from Marissa and Helen's building. Marissa, no longer pregnant, would step out onto the ledge, face-forward. Mirabelle would wait for Marissa's body to hit the pavement.

"But it never does." She shook her shoulders, shedding the idea from her skin. "She just stands there; it feels like hours."

I set the notebook next to me on the bed.

"I just thought that by writing her name down, somehow . . ." She combed her bottom lip with her straight top teeth, recently freed from braces; her lips were chapped because of this habit. "It's probably exactly the kind of shit she wants me to do," she said, meaning her mother. "Which is why I'm giving it to you."

"I don't think dead girls are quite what Sylvia had in mind." We called our mothers by their first names only in their absence. We were still good girls then, but even if we'd been brave enough to try, we wouldn't have known what to rebel against.

Mirabelle smiled wickedly, grabbed the notebook, and held it to her chest. "I hadn't thought of that."

All we had to do was open up the newspaper to see that girls disappeared and died like stray cats. The names stacked up in Mirabelle's notebook easily, effortlessly: hit-and-runs, dog attacks, heart conditions, smothering by an older brother or stepfather who just couldn't stand the girl anymore. We understood that most of the girls were different from us—less comfortable, mostly not white. The distance from danger was further for us, but that year we pretended it wasn't.

We began passing the notebook back and forth, slipping it into each other's knapsacks between classes every few weeks. Over the next nine months, the book's spine cracked and its corners rounded from being shoved between our textbooks and under our mattresses, from being thumbed through on boring Saturday afternoons. Recording the names felt as inevitable as our summer salamander hunts or the spring we'd imagined the trees behind our houses hid witches and trolls when we were younger.

On one gray Saturday afternoon in January, at our usual corner booth at the diner, Mirabelle flipped through the out-of-date jukebox while we waited for our food. Through the window, I watched three boys climb out of a car in the parking lot.

A girl had been shot in a church in California, and Mirabelle, who had the notebook last, had added her name to the list.

"I thought we were sticking to New York," I said, and took a sip of the milk shake we were sharing. The icy bits at the bottom made me shiver.

"Said who?"

Across the table, her chin in her hand, Mirabelle's eyes followed the young men as they goofed around in the parking lot.
They clipped each other's shoulders and mussed each other's
hair. It used to be easy to get Mirabelle to agree with me; she
never bothered to test my temper. But even as her growing dis-
interest in the world alarmed her parents, I'd noticed something
else: She was less and less afraid.

"We need parameters," I said. We had just learned the word
in physical science, and I knew Mirabelle had been spacing out
in class lately, drawing overlapping stars on the rims of her
sneakers during lab.

"Parameters," I repeated. "Rules."

Mirabelle turned back from the window. The boys were on
the front steps now; they'd straightened up and quieted down,
adjusting their hair back into place. I knew it was Mirabelle
who had caught their attention as she stared dreamily out the
window, her cheeks rosy, her light lashes making her seem delicate, precious. I was, you could say, conventionally pretty, with
hair that fell straight and sensibly halfway down my back, a few
shades dirtier than Mirabelle's halolike blond. I scared boys
then, the way I met their eyes. Mirabelle had a way of disappearing with her body that only made you more aware of her
presence. She was doing this now for them: the shifting carefully in her seat, letting her eyes fall on theirs only for a moment
before she looked away.

Neither of us had much in the way of bodies then. We took
each rounding of something that was once flat and bony as a sign
that we were chosen, each pricking up of another consciousness

in the world as a small affirmation. Of course we wanted to be desired.

I motioned for the book with impatient fingers as the boys were led to a table past ours. I began a list of the rules on the page across from Yvonne and Sierra Jeffries, five and seven, abandonment and starvation; and Paulina Krokos, twelve, car crash. We'd keep the dead girls' names, their ages, and a brief description of how they died. Accidents counted, as did murders and suicides, of course. Eventual deaths—the fallout of beatings or multiple drug overdoses that weakened and failed a girl's organs—were tricky, and the rule was, if you went into the hospital following whatever had happened and you never left except through the morgue, it counted, no matter how long it took to die. The girls had to be under eighteen because above this they were women, and subject to another world of danger we weren't ready to fathom.

We divided the Bronx by zip code: 10471, 10463, 10468. We'd take Inwood, which was technically Manhattan. Our borders were defined by the reaches of the number 1 and the 10 buses, farther out into the borough than we'd ever been, but seemingly within our reach. Eventually, we'd take in Yonkers and 10467, the neighborhood where our fathers had met as boys.

By the time we finished the rules, the streetlights were coming on along Broadway. We waited to be picked up in the diner's vestibule, secured by our winter coats, rewrapped in our scarves. I wore Mirabelle's gloves—I had forgotten mine—and she shoved her hands in her coat pockets, chewing a toothpick, leaning against the one mirrored wall. The parking-lot boys were leaving, too. *Excuse me,* they said, one after the other, as they passed through the space. We weren't in their way, but they let their jackets brush against ours. They lingered, waiting for one of us to respond, or to blush, which was usually Mirabelle's job, but she wasn't in the mood.

At school that March the boys had a new game: sticking all manner of sharp objects—sewing needles, freshly sharpened pencils—into the backs of girls' thighs while we walked up the stairs in front of them. Most of us were resigned to the snickering of the boys, who'd slip the objects back up their shirtsleeves and smile with a shit-eating grin if you turned around and looked at them. But when the point of Julian Wilson's compass went into Mirabelle's ass, she didn't yelp, as most of us had been doing for weeks. Mirabelle and I had been coming up the narrower southern stairs from gym. The boys behind us were from the rowdier classes on the other side of the building, the boys you least wanted at your back. They were in eighth grade, too, but many were bigger, some of them having been left behind, and the others—the small and cagey ones—were worse than the slow-moving dumb ones. Julian was one of those smaller ones, popular for being bad, considered handsome by some girls, but not by us.

Mirabelle stopped on the stairs, turning to face Julian. "Stop fucking pricking me."

"What?" Julian looked at her as though she were crazy.

"I said stop fucking poking me with your fucking compass."

Mirabelle tried to fix her face into an ugly expression, but she always looked pretty, even when angry.

Julian smiled politely, and took one step up toward Mirabelle. He leaned in as close to her face as he could without touching her, his dark, pouty lower lip looking as though it might graze Mirabelle's chin.

"I wouldn't stick shit in your"—and here Julian looked around, to make sure the other boys were watching what he was about to do—"skinny. White. Ass."

I stood just behind Mirabelle's right shoulder, facing a crowd of boys with whom I'd barely felt brave enough to make eye contact for the past two years. Their sudden laughter made me flinch. But not Mirabelle; the heat rising from her body wasn't embarrassment, but a tiny thrill.

The buzzer sounded for fifth period. Neither Mirabelle nor Julian moved.

"Boo," Julian said, before pushing his way past her, leading the boys up the stairs to class.


Two weeks after school let out, junior high already a memory we were both trying to forget, the day was sticky hot. Mirabelle and I took the bus to a carnival where the old Pathmark had been. We rode the Spider first, delighting in the grip of the floor loosening under the soles of our sneakers, in our bodies rising up from under the safety bars. We screamed like children.

Perhaps it was the heat that drew us to the Himalaya, whose backdrop was painted to look like a wall of ice, a scene of polar caps and polar bears. Music blared continuously from the ride's central speakers, drowning out the fair games' bells and whirrs. When it was our turn, our hips banged against each other's, against the metal sides of the car, as we rode the Himalaya forward and backward, our car swinging wildly with our lightness, our heads snapping back as the ride changed direction.

We rode three times in a row when the lines were short, and a boy came by to collect our tickets, wilted by our sweaty hands, after each go. He smiled at Mirabelle sideways, and she smiled back, a flush rising up to the dip of her tank top. When we'd had enough, we lifted the bar and stood, our knees buckling; we fell into one another. Mirabelle hooked her elbow into mine and we tried to walk normally down the ramp, but after we passed through the gate the boy held open for us, Mirabelle said, "I don't feel so well."

I left her on a bench along the side of the children's roller coaster while I went to get her something cold to drink. When I returned with a large lemonade, she was on her back, an arm draped over her face.

"She okay?" asked another boy from the Himalaya; he'd sat inside the deejay booth. He was well groomed though not particularly handsome, but he had intense blue eyes and dark lashes. They were blinking on me.

"She'll be fine."

He lit a cigarette, asked, "This okay?"

"Sure," I said.

He took a few drags while Mirabelle hogged the drink. My throat felt dry, but asking her for a sip seemed mean.

"What's your name?" he asked me, stomping out the half-smoked cigarette with a clean sneaker.

I smiled at him, squinting against the chalky white sky. I didn't know if I should tell the truth.

"Nicole," Mirabelle answered for me, and I wanted to stick an elbow in her ribs.

"You live around here, Nicole?"

"Up the hill." I nodded in the direction of our houses.

"Oh, up there, huh?" He pointed his chin up Riverdale Avenue, and it seemed like a faraway land, an inestimable climb.

"You?"

"Jersey." He waited for me to respond, but I just nodded. "But I work all week. You girls coming back here tonight?" Mirabelle rattled the ice cubes in the drink. "Because my cousin's coming by. We could get you in for free." We weren't allowed to go to the fair at night.

"We have to go," Mirabelle said, sucking up the last of the lemonade.

"You feel better?" I asked her.

"I feel fine," she said, rising.

"I'm Josh, by the way," he called out after us as Mirabelle, her hand sticky on my wrist, led me back toward the rides.

"Good-bye, Josh," Mirabelle said just to me.

The rain was light at first, the red and yellow bulbs at the top of the Zipper brilliant against the pale gray sky. But then a single flash of lightning, and a rumble of thunder, and the rides were shut off one by one. They rounded us up like sheep and shooed us out in groups, handing us tickets for a full day as compensation.

Because of the lemonade, we were a dollar short for bus fare home. We spent our change calling Mirabelle's mom from the gas station on the corner, and then mine, but neither of them was home, so we walked. Mirabelle's hoop earrings, which the guy had made her take off before getting on the Gravitron, jingled in her pockets. She put them back in as we walked uphill. The rain curled the ends of Mirabelle's hair into semi-circles, pulling it away from her ears, where the hoops shone bright against her neck.

Two blocks from the top of the hill, a good mile from home, our sneakers were soaked, our bare feet blistering against their slick, rubbery insides. My shorts kept bunching up against the backs of my thighs. I suggested we hitchhike.

"Go ahead," Mirabelle dared me. She started walking faster, looking up at the sky as if it would suddenly stop raining.

I stuck my thumb out on the corner of Greystone and 239th, mostly because I knew Mirabelle would be a little scared if I did. Before either of us could regret my boldness, a blue sedan pulled over. The driver, a woman, motioned us inside, the auto-unlock of the doors like gates being opened. Mirabelle opened the back door, leaving me the front seat. The woman cleared bags and papers onto the floor for me.

"Thank you," I said, surprised my plan had worked, and that we had landed in exactly the kind of car our mothers would be relieved to see us in.

"Oh, please, I had to. This weather . . ." She was younger than she had first appeared to be through the rain-streaked window. No wedding ring, raspy voice.

Mirabelle slid into the backseat next to the woman's two

girls, who unbuckled and re-buckled their seatbelts accordingly. The older one eyed us warily, embarrassed by what her mother had done. But Mirabelle was doll pretty, and when she checked to make sure the clasp was closed on her hoops, their little mouths opened with awe.

"Those are pretty," the smaller one said, reaching up to stick her fingers into the earring's diameter.

At the turn before our houses, the woman said, "Look, I know I shouldn't be saying this, considering I picked you up and all that, but you girls should be careful with this kind of thing. There are a lot of creeps around here."

"We don't usually . . . we've never. . . . ," I began.

"We know," Mirabelle said, smiling apologetically at the woman in the rearview mirror.

Later, in front of my bedroom mirror, we pushed our shorts off our hips and compared the size of our bruises from the ride: Mine was a lemon; Mirabelle's, a peach.

That night, after the storm cleared and the fair reopened, someone dropped a knife from the top of the Ferris wheel. It spun and spun and entered Kiara Nelson's skull at a forty-five-degree angle while she waited in line with her father. The blade severed multiple arteries in her brain, sending Kiara into a coma from which she'd never emerge. We weren't allowed to go back to the fair. Not that summer, not ever.


In September Mirabelle's mother found the notebook. As they always had since we were young, our mothers gathered us in one kitchen to scold us.

"Can you tell us why you are doing this?" my mother asked, shaking her head.

We shrugged, one after the other.

"You understand why this is disturbing, don't you?" Mrs. Diehl asked us, her hand on top of the notebook we'd never see again.

Mirabelle fixed her gaze on the marble countertops. I stared at my mother, who refused to meet my eyes.

"Nicole?" Mrs. Diehl came forward to touch my shoulder.

"What?"

"You understand why we're going to have to take this away, right?"

I didn't answer.

"Whose idea was this?" my mother asked. She directed this question at both of us, but her eyes waited on Mirabelle, who, when we were smaller, had always been the first to own up to what we'd done wrong, to cry through her confession of drawing on the walls with crayons or digging up the flowers for a game we'd invented. After, there'd be a private scolding for me at home, during which my mother would say I'd taken advantage of Mirabelle, manipulated her, and that I should be more mindful of my influence over her.

But Mirabelle didn't say anything, and we both waited them out, our arms crossed over our chests, till they sent us out of the room. I didn't get that lecture this time.

Waiting for the 10 bus to school in late November, it felt like it might snow soon. We were only a few stops from school when

Mirabelle suggested we cut. At the high school, the bus driver waited for us to file out with the other kids. He looked at us in his rearview mirror and shook his head silently before letting the doors hiss closed.

When we returned to where we'd started, we slipped our knapsacks under our jackets and walked briskly home. Our parents were at work; we left our bags by my back door and set off on a walk. Leaves, brown and brittle, swirled around our ankles, following us as we walked down the road. I felt happily invisible as we moved deeper into the neighborhood.

As the houses got bigger and the streets got quieter, we came to a house that looked abandoned, in the way only houses in our neighborhood could be: wrapped in tarps and guarded by a construction Dumpster, its renovations on hold for the winter. Mirabelle tried a window along the back side of the house; it opened without a fight. The room we climbed into was filled with a concrete gray light, dark enough to make me wish we had a flashlight, or candles. The house smelled of construction dust and cold, and faintly of the wood from a neighbor's fireplace.

The house was just a shell, its insides ripped out. We snaked through the rooms silently, holding hands. When we got to what was once probably, or was going to be, the kitchen, we sat on the floor, looking out onto the Hudson through the old French doors. There seemed no rush to get anywhere; no one would be looking for us in the place we'd gone.

"I'm thinking of going away," Mirabelle told me then, the first words either of us had spoken since we'd been in the house.

"What do you mean?"

"There's a boarding school in New Hampshire that we're looking at."

"For next fall?"

"No, for January. It's expensive, but my parents think it's better for me," she said, and began to cry.

I looked at her, her knees drawn up to her chest, her fingers turning salmon pink in the cold.

I listened to the trains along the river below, to the cars on Palisade Avenue. I let Mirabelle cry next to me in the cold and empty house, because that is what she wanted to do.


Although her parents went to see her at school two or three times the next semester, I never took the invitations they extended to me to join them. I could tell from her voice during our few phone calls that Mirabelle didn't really want me there, that we both needed the space. We wrote each other letters; mostly I sent her gossip about the kids we knew, and she told me about how bad the food was and what the buildings on campus looked like. Neither of us mentioned the new friends we were making.

Mirabelle came home for the summer while I was still finishing up ninth grade. She had a boyfriend, but not the kind her parents had wanted for her, not some East Coast old-money type but a pale Irish kid from Yonkers named Joseph with a shaved head and a diamond earring. He'd pick her up three blocks from her house in a rumbling Oldsmobile that smelled like a lifetime of smoke. He was somebody from school's cousin's friend. "Not all of them are snobs, you know," she told me. "There are some real people there, too."

I had fallen for a neighborhood boy, one of the kind she would say weren't real, and he wasn't: He had thick, godlike eyebrows, and T-shirts with little rips in them; he went to a private school, and was two grades above me. Every few weeks I let him push me up against his garage and kiss me, his chest a little too strong against mine; I let him make me keep it all a secret. I'd look at him longingly across the driveway as we both helped our parents in the yard on the weekend, waiting for some signal of recognition. He'd concentrate on the grass or the spade in his hand. I wasn't real to him either.

I saw Mirabelle and Joseph riding around one afternoon on Milton Avenue, where I was picking up hamburger meat for my mother from the butcher. At the four-way stop, Mirabelle pulled out a piece of golden hair from her mouth, where it got caught in a laugh. She waved as they turned the corner, her face turning more childlike when she noticed me. I waved back, but I was already looking at the car behind them by then.

Mirabelle came by the house later that night with her mother, who sat with mine at the kitchen table, drinking beer, sun-kissed and loud, as if they were the teenagers. I didn't understand then how they could love each other so unconditionally, how they didn't seem to want or need anyone else, didn't need a little breathing room.

Mirabelle and I sat in the yard, our heels tucked up against our shorts bottoms on the old wood chairs.

"Did you see me today, on Milton? I waved."

I thought about pretending I hadn't, decided not to.

"I did. I waved back, but you were already gone."

"Oh, I didn't see."

"Where were you going?"

"Just around. Just driving."

I picked at the backs of my heels with a fingernail, flaking off hard skin.

"Hey, you should come with us one day," Mirabelle said.

"Sure," I said, but I knew I couldn't stand to be in the backseat of that car, watching his hand cup her shoulder, massage the back of her neck, slink through her hair. It was too goddamned hot to be close to anyone those days, but I knew they did it, knew they pulled over to the shady places and went at it. I could tell by the way Mirabelle moved. She didn't need to tell me herself.

After dinner, we walked over to the park—although it was nearly nine, the night wasn't dark yet. We each took a swing, leaving one between us. The seats bore the memory of the day's sun, swollen and forgiving in their warmth, metal that would have stung our thighs had we let it meet our skin earlier.

I was the first to stand up on the swing, but it was Mirabelle who said, "Contest?" and I said, "Why not?" We began to bend our knees and pump, our hands slippery on the chains, the fence flying up to meet us. We had heard that these sorts of games were dangerous, that if we were to become part of local legend, if other girls were to keep watch over us, one of us must level out with the top of the set, then catapult over the chain-link to the street on the other side, land in a heap of wasted child body, lie in rivers of blood. Be gone. We had heard such things had happened.

# Looking for a Thief

*I am the master of my fate,*
*I am the captain of my soul.*
—William Ernest Henley, "Invictus"

The boys are setting up a tent in the dining room. Margaret, in the kitchen, can hear the chairs squeaking and moaning against the floors, Wesley's exaggerated grunting as Matthew directs the boys to push. After she puts the chicken in the oven, she goes to check on them, rinsing her hands in the sink beforehand. Indeed, the dining room table is now crooked against the far wall, the chairs lined up like executionees on the perimeter. In the middle, a tent she and Ian camped in a long time ago, sun bleached and ratty, at half-mast. The boys rigged it to the legs of the dining room table; it worked well enough to hold them. Its opening faces the window, outside which snow steadily falls. It has been snowing for three days, through the weekend, and now, Monday, a snow day from school.

Wesley's socks are unmatched, and one of them, likely belonging to Jonas, flops off the tip of his toe. Wesley scratches his nose, surveying the scene. "I don't think that's right," he says, pointing to a corner whose poles bend in the wrong direction. Wesley is the baby, and he has just discovered that he can correct his brothers, and sometimes even be right.

Matthew crawls out from inside the tent on his knees, inspects the corner to which Wesley is still insistently pointing. "Huh," he says, as though it matters, and goes back inside to perform some other operation.

Margaret takes a seat on one of the chairs, and instinctively, Wesley comes to her, pulling himself back onto her knees. She can smell the sweat gathering under his turtleneck, from the thrill, perhaps, of a day spent with his brothers. They watch the other two boys work around the misbehaving pole. Jonas works silently, but Matthew mutters to himself, little *huh*s and *oh*s that don't indicate anything to anyone but him. Both boys push and prod the fabric, its metal parts clanging against one another, against the floor, as the tent is raised and lowered and raised again. Wesley gets up occasionally to stand over Jonas and Matthew, but Margaret can see there is no place for him to insert himself.

Margaret wants to be able to help, to lay the tent on the ground and direct the boys step by step, as she directed Ian so many years ago, but she wouldn't know how to put it together anymore.

When Ian comes home in the navy blue darkness of evening, he slides open the dining room's pocket door; Margaret can hear it moving along its rails from the study, where she is checking her e-mail. No news yet of when the new pages for the cookbook she's testing will arrive, the messengers delayed by the current chaos of public transit, the book's author too temperamental, too paranoid to send it over e-mail.

"Hello in there," she hears Ian call out.

"Hello," the boys reply, each greeting tripping on the end of the one before.

"Whatcha pretending in there?" Ian's spent all day at the airport, trying and failing to get on a flight to Atlanta for a meeting, and she can hear the dislocation in his voice. "Pretending you're out in the tundra? At the North Pole?" he tries. In the moments of the boys' silence an e-mail comes through from the editor: Tomorrow, she's promised, they'll get a messenger to her.

"Yeah," says Jonas, finally, and Margaret envisions her son shrugging as he does so, the tent's fabric bulging out with his shoulder.

The boys came one after the other, a little flood of children that was neither a choice nor a concession. Four years ago, when the boys were little, they lived in Manhattan. She always knew they'd leave. They'd agreed on the move; they'd always agreed on those kinds of things. Ian says he remembers the moment he decided it was enough, when they had all three on the subway one spring morning, the boys sliding around the concave orange seats, the feeling that there weren't enough hands to keep them all in place. They tell these stories for the first year or two after they move to New Jersey, which is barely less expensive, and then they stop thinking of themselves as refugees; they stop explaining. At first, she felt relief: at the just-right amount of space between her and her neighbors, at the fenced yard and the one perfect little school and the other defectors from Brooklyn and Washington

Heights, New York City a mistake they're all supposed to be recovering from. A community re-formed; a life, easier in the ways they had wanted it to be during the boys' early childhood years, took shape.

Margaret has always been able to let go. She doesn't keep things from their past: not their little hospital ID bracelets, or first shoes, or the old MetroCards Jonas used to run along the walls of their apartment, which she'd find in his jacket pockets. Not her wedding invitation or clothes that don't fit anymore. Margaret doesn't keep things but Ian does. That night she's in their bathroom, looking in the vanity for a bar of soap someone brought as a housewarming gift all those years ago, when she finds the box of teeth in a drawer. There are two of these boxes, actually, orange square plastic containers, with hinged lids that snap into place, though there are three children, all of whom have lost teeth, exchanging them for dollar bills they would often lose a few days later.

She walks out into their bedroom, both boxes in one hand. "What the fuck is this?" she asks Ian, laughing.

"I didn't want to throw them out," he says, undoing the buttons on his shirt.

Down the hall, she hears Jonas hacking, a cough he hasn't been able to shake for weeks.

"And what are we doing with them?" She rattles the boxes one by one. "Shit, they're all mixed up, aren't they?"

She can't stop laughing.

He turns a light pink.

"They might want them . . . one day."

"And you'll separate them out?"

"Come on," he says, and turns away from her as he takes off the rest of his clothes.

She bites her lip to keep the laughter from coming, returns to the bathroom. She is about to drop the boxes into the small wastebasket under the sink, but instead puts them back in Ian's side of the vanity, in a drawer with travel-size shaving cream cans and an unopened package of dental floss.

He's under the covers when she gets into bed, turned on his side, reading a work report. If she were feeling kinder, would she suggest they go camping? They used to strip down to nothing in that tent, their skin papery in the cold. He always offered to be on the ground, sliding under her.

*Fun*, is what he says when people ask what it's like to have three boys, the inquirer giving Margaret a sympathetic look, as if wildness cannot be what she is after, too. But she chased Ian, who was older and so confident, even at twenty-five, when she met him. And he always called her that, *fun*. So maybe she's the one who was chased, domesticated. She wanted this. She chose it.

In bed, she puts her hand on the back of his neck; he murmurs his good night, shimmies his body closer to the cast of the bedside light.


Jonas wakes up in the middle of the night, hungry. This happens every few months. He's at their bedroom door, the hall light on behind him. Ian wakes up just to wake her, pokes his fingers into her back. She swings out of bed and takes Jonas by the hand to the kitchen, where both of them recoil at the bright light of the refrigerator. He eats leftover spaghetti, barely warmed in the microwave, in gulps, and then says, "I feel better," before they walk upstairs together and get back into their own beds.

Last week it was Wesley who woke up. When it isn't the growing, the hunger so deep it hurts, it's the blood. No one told her about the blood—not of childbirth, or the return of her period, earlier with every baby, just as she'd had enough of the bodily fluids of others; those cycles women know. News: the split lips, the scrapes, the bloody noses—that beautiful red a Hansel and Gretel crumb trail from the boys' bedroom to theirs, Wesley screaming, his face pressed into her nightshirt till they were both covered. The next morning, she woke up and walked the path back to his bedroom with a damp washcloth, useless against what he'd smeared with the back of his hand on the grain of the wallpaper they'd always planned to remove. At least, she thinks, she does not have girls, will not have waste-baskets overflowing with bloody pads. But girls are taught to be discreet. Boys, who shout their own terror, make a mess of it, take you down with them.

She learned in her sophomore biology seminar that attachment is just another way into survival, another of biology's brilliant tricks. Then, that understanding that the female body is designed for reproduction, for sustaining at its own cost and peril, for simply carrying on that set of cycles, drove her to the campus health clinic to request birth control pills. She had no boyfriend; there was no casual sex. *No*, she wanted to say to her body, to work against it. She was nineteen. And then, only ten years after that seminar, a shift. A yes.

By the second and third pregnancies the magic was gone but not the power. The power felt more natural by then. Ian used to say, especially in front of the boys, that a pregnant woman would do anything to keep a baby alive. "Even kill the daddy," he'd joke, Matthew delighting in this idea, asking Margaret if she really would.

"Probably," she said one morning at breakfast, considering. She touched her belly under the lip of the table, reminding herself. It was easy to forget at five months in, with Wesley then, that she was pregnant. The body took over. It didn't matter at that point whether she wanted the baby, if she'd care for him after, if she would love him. The baby would grow and be born and either of them might die in that—especially she—and then everything within her would go to keeping the baby alive, to keeping herself alive, to healing, so she could do it again.

But every few months, Margaret leans into Ian's ear and says of one of the boys, "Look at what we did. We made a fucking person," remembering only the miracles of biology, what to be grateful for.

At breakfast the next morning, before they sort through the pile of hats and gloves and boots for the walk through the snow to the bus stop, knee-high where it's been plowed to the sidewalk's edges, the boys eat their cereal and toast quietly, as if still in the land of dreams, as if still in the tent. Matthew and Jonas can break back into this world, but not, Margaret sees, Wesley. He is the sleeper of the group, and she had to rouse him over and over again this morning. The other boys are done with breakfast, with getting dressed and packing their school bags. Ian left for the airport in darkness, his alarm, though it vibrated, waking her, too, at 4:15, but she wasn't able to fall back asleep.

"Come on now," she says to Wes, who has only pushed his fingers into his toast. "Time to start eating."

"I want to stay home," he says, his face crumpling, the tiny bite of toast he conceded muffling his sentence. She looks away from his open mouth, sips her coffee.

"You can't," she says, calling him honey, apologizing. "I have to work."

"I can be quiet," he says, through tears.

"You have to go to school," she says.

He slams his fist on the table, screams, "I! WANT! TO! STAY! HOME!"

"It's not a choice."

"Yes it is," he says.

"You have to go and you have to stop crying," she says.

"No!" Wesley pushes his plate across the table. "I will not stop crying."

"Then out," she says, pointing to the yard. "You can't do that in here."

He goes; he's always followed instructions. She picks up his plate and lets it land, loudly, in the sink.

She's harder on him than she was on the others, because he's the last one, because he wasn't really wanted, because she is harder because of that fact. And she knows, she believes five-year-old boys can cry. That they should. But that kind of grace isn't hers to give this morning, and she leaves him out there, in a protracted weep, shutting the glass door on him so she hears him less as she loads the dishwasher. She needs to use her hands, even as they are clumsy, as last night's wineglasses feel slippery and fragile between her fingers. They don't break. Outside, Wesley stomps his feet, throws his head back, but she barely looks in the direction of the yard. The neighbors can hear, she is sure. She leaves the door unlocked, and goes out to get him when he bangs on it so hard she thinks it might break. They have to go, anyway.

They've missed the school bus by now. After she drops them off, she finds herself driving, mindlessly, around the jagged outline of the town park, past the houses they admired and quickly learned they couldn't afford. The train station wasn't close enough, anyway. She has tried this before, going for a drive, but it does not help. There is nothing mind clearing about knowing you could drive forever, for days, for weeks, and not land anywhere far enough away from your own life to pretend you can even imagine other choices.

In the city, they didn't have a car. When she needed to be alone, she would undo all the locks and sit outside in the building hallway, just outside the door, the chain stuffed between the door and the frame. The floor was dirty, but it was cool, and it was outside. If one of the boys asked her where she was—always Jonas—she'd say she was throwing out the trash and wash her hands at the sink when she was discovered missing. But they rarely did. When she did go out with the trash or recycling, really, did they worry she wouldn't return? The thought never even crossed their minds.

A day after the boys go back to school the tent still stands in the dining room. She dismantles it late in the morning when she should be working, but the power is wonky, and she needs the kitchen outlets. The lights flicker on the south side of the house; in Manhattan, the lines were buried, and she is not used to this pausing, still, after four years. When she goes into the garage she turns the circuit on and off, but it doesn't help. She leaves it alone. She puts the tent on the hood of the car to do this. Her car lives in the garage; Ian's is at the end of the driveway, near the small curb. He shovels it out every winter without complaining, at least to her. The hood of her car is cold but clear of snow; they got it in on time. The trick was shoveling the pile in front of the garage door so there would be a path to drive out into.

She puts the tent in the trunk of her car—not in the attic, where it was, or in the basement, where it will be easier to find when they need it next. But what if she needs it next? It's a just-in-case move, in and of itself ridiculous; she wouldn't go live in a tent. But she might. She could. The important thing to remember is that she could. The tent folds up so nicely, sits so unobtrusively in the top left corner of the trunk. You can put groceries on top of it. A pile of ice skates or jackets cast aside because it's too warm inside or outside, because you have miscalculated. The jackets with the names of their brothers written in on the neck. Their shared last name, not hers. The tent sits so unobtrusively she will forget about it. Then it's Thursday, and she picks them up at school in the car because she's already out, getting a set of ingredients she forgot to buy yesterday, and she's close to school. How the boys love to be picked up; how they love to get in a warm car, though at first she insisted, after the move, that they'd walk to school. That was why they moved to this town, wasn't it, to pretend they were not giving up all that much.

She takes their backpacks into the front seat next to her. Matthew is in the middle, Jonas behind her, Wesley behind the passenger's seat. She waits for them to buckle. She asks how their day was, and two of the three mumble, "Good."

"Nothing exciting, huh?" she asks as they wait to exit the carpool line.

Jonas says, "There was a lockdown today."

Here they all are, unharmed, behind her. No phone calls, no news vans.

"A drill?" she asks. Twice a year they do these, practice playing dead in the classroom. Before the older boys can answer, the little one says, "They were looking for a thief."

She catches the older one's eye in the mirror. "Do not," she says. And he doesn't.

"They had to check the whole building," Wesley says, making his hands large in his lap.

"Big building," she says.

"It took, like, four hours," he says.

"And then we had gym," says Jonas.

Gym class, the second-to-last block of the day. Some days, his face is still a touch pink when he comes home.

"They didn't find him," Wesley says.

She takes them to the bakery in town, where she buys

herself a coffee and each of them a doughnut; feeding everyone is the only thing that comes to mind. It's already dark, not even five o'clock. The coffee will keep her awake tonight. Half-decaf, she remembers to ask for. Wesley keeps asking why they're getting specials, which is what he calls sweets, a word Margaret and Ian tried to use to talk around the older boys some years ago, negotiating their quiet and calm over their heads. No one answers Wes to his satisfaction. He doesn't finish his doughnut, offers the rest of it to Margaret and the other two boys, who both shake their heads no. Matthew knocks his lukewarm hot chocolate across the tabletop onto both his brothers, soaking Jonas's pants and Wesley's coat, which he crumpled next to him.

"Let's just get home," she says to them when Jonas starts to whine about the mess, gagging over the smell of the sugary milk, even as the word feels false in her mouth. Margaret is from California, and nothing has felt close to home in decades, not New York, where they both wanted to live but neither loved, and not this sensible town in New Jersey. Home is just the house, with its shiny black door and brass knocker that no one is permitted to use for the way it echoes throughout the first floor, for the noise they want to make for the sake of making noise. She doesn't regret the choice to stay east but wishes she might, that there might be another opportunity they haven't taken. She holds the idea of that open the way she used to hold open the possibilities of her and Ian's future together: what they'd do, where they'd live, their children, how many and when and their names, all the banal facts of their family. What she misses is that feeling of possibility, the unknowing.

Now the unknowing is for the boys, their futures, lives she

wants them to take over as soon as they can. But she does not want to go back to the before, even into the illusion of it. She understands she is owed nothing.

That night after the boys are in bed, Margaret tells Ian, back from his trip, about sending Wesley out into the yard the other morning.

"I feel bad," she says as they pull fresh sheets on the bed from opposite sides of the mattress.

"He won't remember it," he reassures her. "You did fine."

She knows he is right. Wesley would remember the things that make him want to be with her, again, tomorrow.

"More snow tonight," Ian says in the dark bedroom. He's exhausted, asleep in minutes.

Everyone sleeps through the night, even Margaret. The snow comes, but school is still on, though Ian's office is closed; it's worse, apparently, in Manhattan. He takes the boys to the bus stop, not even wearing a coat. He works from home, pacing the study while on a phone call, arms crossed over his chest at the window. She watches him from the hallway, a stack of recipes in her hands, notes the way his tongue rests on his bottom lip, waiting for a way into the conversation. She never gets to see this part of Ian, the working part, the thinking, the strategizing. The parts she doesn't need to hold in herself to be with him. He doesn't notice her in the hall, and she leaves before he can. In the kitchen, she scrubs three pounds of potatoes for a gratin she's certain no one will like but that she'll serve on the side of dinner; the weather hasn't moved her deadlines. She takes an afternoon shower while the gratin's in the oven and offers to be the one who waits out at the corner for the bus to show up, though her hair is still wet, though the bus is taking longer than it usually does.

She touches each of the boys as they come off the bus, but Wes is the only one who takes her hand, though he releases it shortly after so he can scratch his nose.

When they come in the house it's as though she hasn't seen Ian all day, and she hasn't, really. And he looks new and unfamiliar, home in the afternoon light on a weekday, his sweatshirt hood pulled up as he, too, comes into the kitchen looking for a snack. She shows the boys how her hair has frozen out in the afternoon wind, encourages them to crack the strands into warmth again, into wet. A few hours after she falls asleep that night, she wakes up, imagining she hears the boys, asking for her, but it's another house noise; four years and she hasn't learned all of them yet.

Late Saturday morning, Ian drives her to the train station, the one a bit farther from the house, because it's a better line to be on. The boys are headed to a movie at the library, out to lunch, the day packed with plans while she spends hers in Manhattan with a friend.

"Stop!" Jonas says from the backseat. "Stop!"

"Four! Fivesixseveneightniiiiiine!" shouts Wesley.

"He's counting!" Jonas whines.

"So what?" says Ian. "Let a dude count."

Wesley rambles on, numbers falling from his mouth at random.

"It's annoying," Jonas says, smacking his own thigh in frustration.

"Flower sign!" Wesley shouts as they pass a highway memorial. She is glad he doesn't ask what they are. Ian doesn't like to lie to him, and his brothers know. When Matthew first heard about death, it was months of night wakings and tantrums, of impossible questions: *Will you be with me when I die? Who is going to die first, me or Jonas or Daddy? Will the dirt get into my eyes?*

One of her friends who stayed in the city takes every opening to remind her of the danger of driving. *Be careful*, she says, as though Margaret is not.

Margaret doesn't say anything as the boys continue to argue. She should have gone to the other station, the transfers now seeming worth it. She waves good-bye to the boys in the backseat ("Where are you going?" Jonas, only now, asks), touches Ian's knee as she gets out of the car. "Good luck," she says in parting.

Lunch with her friend, Caroline, is gossip about their old neighborhood, where neither of them lives nor visits anymore, discussions about who has stuck around too long, who is doing better than expected, who is leaving for a job or school or the Midwestern city they grew up in. They write down the titles of books for one another, the names of doctors, brands of mascara. Caroline makes inappropriate jokes about the waiter working the other side of the restaurant, blond and chisel jawed. She asks after the boys. Margaret waves the talk of them away. The usual. They drink coffee and Bloody Marys.

Caroline is considering, again, quitting her job, whether she can, what could be next.

"You thinking of doing something from home?" Margaret asks.

"I don't know. That's hard, still, right?"

"Always," Margaret says.

It's been so long since the neighborhood playgroup where they met, and they don't lie to each other, not then, especially not now. On her last trip into the city Margaret ran into one of the other women from that group, Amy, who still lived in the neighborhood, but she confessed as they rode from Twenty-third Street downtown that she, too, was curious about New Jersey. She asked about the real estate and the schools, which Margaret described as honestly as she could: the work of a house, the unevenness of the classroom teachers, the evening traffic something she forgot existed. "But you're happy," Amy insisted as they were squeezed closer together by another pack of commuters. For Amy, who'd had so much trouble breastfeeding she'd endured bleeding nipples for the first two months of her baby's life, Margaret answered yes that day on the train, because it was the answer she wanted, because Amy must be someone else beyond those first feral months they spent together in rooms full of toys and half-eaten bagels, someone else she doesn't really know, and this is how you talk to strangers.

Margaret relays the story about Amy, whom she and Caroline called Saint Amy, after Catherine or Agatha, whichever saint it was who bled in the same way, torture. Caroline rolls her eyes.

"She's sweet," says Margaret.

"She's always heard just what she wants to."

Margaret's phone, resting on the table, vibrates three times. "Go ahead," her friend says. She still has a baby at home, and a husband who counts the hours she's away, one of the ones who keep score.

*Boys want to put tent up again.*

*Looked in basement/their room. Did I miss it?*

*Arg.*

Margaret quickly taps out: *Don't know, sorry love*, and puts her phone back into her coat pocket. "Ian, looking for something," she says to her friend.

"Dear God, every last one of them does that, don't they?" Caroline says.

Then, while her friend is in the bathroom, Margaret, a full Bloody Mary in her, types: *Try the trunk, my car. Long story.*

She holds the phone in her hand, waiting. She licks the salt, pink and expensive and mineral, from the rim of the glass, rubs it into the pockets of her cheeks with her tongue.

He sends back a face with its tongue out, its eyes closed. *Weirdo*, he says.

The server takes her empty glass before she can take more salt. She orders two more for her and Caroline. "Catch up," she says, when her friend returns from the bathroom.

*When are you back?* he texts half an hour later. She pretends she doesn't see it, not till she is already on her way home.


On Sunday, after the boys have been tucked in bed, Margaret does the dishes, the warm water an antidote to the drafty window over the sink, to the cold tile floors. Ian calls her name from the study. She keeps washing, waiting for him to come to her. She can hear the boys still settling into bed, the floor creaking as they turn off the lights, pull blankets up over their shoulders, down to cover their feet. The house already feels small; sound carries.

Ian calls her name again, and she turns off the water at the sound of worry in his voice. In the study, he's standing away from the computer, hands on his hips, like how he watches Matthew's flag football games.

"Did you read that e-mail," he asks, pointing at the computer, "from the school?"

"The one about the lockdown?"

"You did."

"The boys told me, when I picked them up."

"Why didn't you tell me?"

"It was already over."

The e-mail is three days old. One line about a false report of a perpetrator on campus, the rest an assurance of a plan. Margaret deleted it when it came through, seeing it was a slightly modified version of the one they received with the safety protocols—fire, weather, shooters—at the start of every year.

"You're on the list," she says.

"They're never important."

He presses his fingers to his forehead, exhales loudly.

She thinks of all the things he has not told her: the time Wes lost a sneaker to a muddy pond, and she'd looked for it at home for nearly an hour before calling him at work, thinking she was losing her mind; his uncle's bone cancer; parties he promised them to and groceries they ran out of. But, really, had she wanted to know those things? Did they seem, once she did know, like secrets? She knows so well the burden of being told, of knowing, and how impossible it is to unknow, to forget. The tent and gym class and thieves.

"It's so fucked up," he says.

She could say, *You didn't think we'd be safe here, did you?* but he'd think she was calling him a fool, which, really, she is. But she understands, too, that someone in the family has to be the one who forgets just enough every now and then, so they can keep moving forward.

She pulls his hand from his forehead, closes it in both of hers. "I know."

They stand like this, in front of the old couch in the study, till his thumb starts to move against her palm, and she steps toward him, and takes his other hand, too.

# Red Light, Green Light

"**D**o you trust me?" the boy asked.

I said yes, though it meant the opposite. Yes meant no I do not. Yes meant this is why we are here, because you are in eighth grade and the schoolyard is no place for surrender.

Arturo shook his head and licked his thumb, used it to wipe something from the point of my chin—"I don't know what that is," he said—and this act drew the teacher over to us, where she saw his hand, returned, lower, to my knee, and he sold me out. "She asked me to," he said.

"What for?" my mother asked the next morning as she dialed the aunt who promised to watch me while she worked. "The attention?" This was my second suspension since I started sixth grade; this time, they gave me three days.

I narrowed my eyes at her but only when her back was to me. Arturo had not been suspended, but for the next week he'd be kept inside at recess with an aide and a book. He liked to read; he was probably happy.

The teacher who caught us said, "Boys will be boys." When my mother recapped the story for my aunt later that evening on the phone, down to the nasal tittering of the teacher as she delivered that line, she added, "Because they don't know my daughter."

The look she gave the teacher in the office that afternoon was harder than the one she gave me as she motioned for me to get my bag. Some days—nights, mostly—she could be tender with me, but that, too, was from a kind of exhaustion, the other side of another failed solution.

On this morning in the kitchen, we all listen to the phone ringing and ringing at my aunt's house. I braid my sister's hair because my mother doesn't have the patience or the fingers for it. I tie off the ends with purple rubber bands, tap the top of her head to let her know she is free to go, but she lingers for a moment between my knees before she snaps back to attention and walks to the sink with the glass of milk she's been drinking.

My mother puts the phone back on the receiver. She looks at me the same way she has been scowling at an empty patch of grass in the park down the block—she knows something is off, but not what, exactly. I know. They cut down a tree, a birch that had been there since I could remember. They even carted the stump away. I wouldn't tell her. She'd have to figure it out herself.

# Second-Chance Family

Twice a week I pick up my half sister's kids from school while she goes to various appointments: therapy, a midwife, a waxing salon. The children aren't mine so I feed them cookies. I wipe the crumbs from the cracks of their lips with my thumb, then let them drop onto the floor of the subway car. I find a crushed Hydrox in my bag when I'm out one night; I make the man I'm on a third date with lick the crumbs from my fingers, a test he fails. I do not wipe his lips. I do not see him again. Good riddance. Adieu. The man of my dreams can live with some cookie crumbs, especially if they are from someone else's children.

It's Thursday, one of our regular days, and my mother, who comes into the city every six or so weeks, is annoyed that I still have to go help Jill. I am the daughter of my father's second-chance family, the one he tried after he failed with his first. He named me Hope. I am, depending on who is asking, an only child, or the youngest of four, two half sisters and one half brother, all so grown now that they're already at work on not replicating their parents' mistakes. I am twenty-four.

We're in the elevator going down from my apartment, a studio my parents bought as an investment—not that I have asked for it, not that I feel like the space belongs to me any more than it would if I rented it. When my mother comes to see me, her bag always contains the same things: the same black cashmere cardigan and slim dark-wash jeans, the same travel-size shampoos and creams she lays out along the back of the sink, though she's only here for forty-eight hours. We sleep on the queen bed that used to be in my teenage bedroom, both of us turned toward the respective walls that are less than a foot away. She doesn't like museums or shopping, but ever since she stopped working downtown last year, she misses walking Manhattan, and so this is what she does while I am at work: puts on a good pair of sneakers and expensive sunscreen and covers a neighborhood. She asks me about whether this or that place is still there or there yet, but the way it is in New York, half the time she's talking about what has disappeared: shops and restaurants and buildings I never knew existed to start with, the overlapping of all the versions of this island we once inhabited as a family. Just before I started sixth grade we moved to the suburbs, another way for them to try something new, something separate from what hadn't worked for my father the first time around.

Before the elevator doors open, my mother hands me my tea, which she's been holding for me as I put my keys back into my bag, and exhales loudly. "I made a commitment," I remind her, but she was never the one who was particular about sticking by her word; that is my father, who has always admired follow-through.

I don't tell her today is for Jill's prenatal yoga; no one knows about the pregnancy yet, not my father or Jill's mother or Caitlin or Jack. Jill is almost in the clear, she says, a few more weeks, though her belly has popped; last week she lifted her shirt to show me her unbuttoned pants, held together by a grocery-store rubber band. *This*, she said, *will happen to you*, and drew a circle around her belly with a flourish. I didn't even look down, so accustomed to Jill's undressing in front of me, to the nakedness that seems to always happen at that house between the children and Jill's constant motion from one part of her life to another, which always requires something else to wear. *Aunting, best birth control ever, right? Use a condom tonight!* she shouted after me as I left that evening. I had a date with the crumb hater.

As we step out of the lobby, my mother puts on her sun-glasses. "It's beautiful out, isn't it?" she says, not wanting an answer. "I'll find us a place for dinner. Six?"

"Six is good," I say, and we both walk off into our days.

The kids know about the baby. Anjali figured it out, Jill says, just by looking at her face. "She said it looked different, and then asked me if I was pregnant," Jill told me, shaking her head, widening her eyes. "That little freak." Anjali is nine. She is currently fascinated by how everything eats: fetuses and the tiny crabs they found on the beach last summer and the snake in the classroom down the hall.

That afternoon on the train platform, Anjali tells me about the placenta; I grit my teeth, try not to make faces. I have never been good with blood. As she talks, her hands grip an imaginary pulsating cord. Sacha, her brother, leans into my legs, presses his fingertips into the holes of my belt. He has a cold; his breathing is heavy. His small shoulders aren't wide enough to hold his backpack; it slides off.

"Enough, okay?" I say to Anjali.

"Does it make you sick?" she asks.

"A little."

"It's just science."

"Well, sometimes science is gross."

I reach for her hand when the train pulls in, Sacha still clinging to my lower half, and we squeeze our way into a car; I find seats for them. Though they are dark haired like me, like their father, no one mistakes them for mine.

"Don't lean on strangers," I say to Sacha, and he sits upright, blinking at the woman next to him, whom he's been using as a wall, who gives me a smile to say it's okay. It's amazing to me how kind people are to children, the grace they're offered, even at their most feral. But both of these children are beautiful, with icy blue eyes rimmed in impossibly dark lashes. People, women especially, stop us on the street to say as much, waiting for a gratitude that the kids don't understand and that I, having nothing to do with it, cannot offer. Anjali complains about this attention. When she was younger, she used to shut her eyes, but the laughter of the admirers would just make her more upset.

I have to keep righting Sacha the whole way.

I will stay with the kids when the baby comes. It's not that

I live the closest, but that they like me the best, Jill says. "Caitie's, well, you know," she says, using a nickname for our sister that I've never felt close enough to her to use myself, even though we lived together for a few years, when I was younger and she was in high school. I *don't* know; I don't want to know. I've learned that my best position in these conversations, when I'm in them, is a simple "mmmm," which can later be construed as neither agreement nor defense. My family, in any of its incarnations, doesn't have enough neutrality.

Once inside the house, Sacha transfers from my leg to his mother's. I hand her his backpack, which I've been carrying for him.

"He can carry it home," she says, not unkindly. "He should."

"I think he's sick," I say to her.

"Yeah, a little," she says, cupping the side of his face. "A month into the school year and already, colds."

Anjali has abandoned her backpack in the doorway from the foyer to the family room; she's taken her shoes off but left them a distance apart from one another across the threshold, socks balled up shortly afterward. "Can I have a snack?" she calls from the kitchen.

"One minute," Jill calls back. She traces the trail of dropped objects with her finger and rolls her eyes at me. "I have clothes for you," she says, waving me inside. "A big bag."

There are always bags of clothes ready for me to look through in a corner of her closet, though we're not built the same. I go home and try on the clothes, the dresses and tops (we both know the pants will be too short on me), imagining myself into some other life; not hers—mother, museum administrator, woman who knows actual artists—but not mine, which is empty of possibility in both the work and love departments. The clothes don't look like castoffs—Jill has always taken care of her things—but they feel that way against my body, even when they fit. They feel impossible, full of something I haven't yet earned. I pass most of them on to a friend, a writer, who doesn't look like Jill at all either, but whom the clothes suit so well that when I see them on her, it's as though Jill has entirely disappeared from them.

For the first few weeks I picked up the kids for her, Jill tried to press cash into my hand on my way out, but I didn't let her. I do need the money but I prefer our relationship to be free. *Dinner?* she'll ask now on my way out, as if it's a new idea, though she offers every Thursday. Some nights I stay and some nights I lie. *Date*, I'll say, or *Plans*, or *Exhausted*. Jill knows when I'm doing it, and she lets it go, so I always come back.

"My mom's in," I say, and she nods. "Cool. Tell her I say hi."

Back underground I go.

My mother likes this Mediterranean place a few blocks from my apartment. When I get there, she's at a table reading a book, half a piece of bread absentmindedly in one hand. I put the bag of clothes against my side, by the wall. She was not even thirty when she married my father, and maybe she'd do it differently now, but then she thought it best to keep a healthy distance between herself and my half siblings. *They don't need a mother; they don't want a mother,* she used to say, even as she criticized the parenting of their actual mother, Emily, the wildness of Jill and Jack up through their early thirties, Caitlin's distrusting nature. *Like living with a sad little ghost*, Mom has said of the years Caitlin lived with us.

"I'm starving," she tells me without looking up.

I am, too, and we order.

Over dinner, she convinces me to play hooky from work the next day to hang out with her. "Take a day. Enjoy this weather before it's gone." It's been unseasonably warm, a last bit of summer even though it officially ended two weeks ago.

"I do need new glasses," I say. "Maybe we can do that?" Whenever she is in town, I find things to ask her for advice on—which shoes to wear that day, whether I should paint a wall—because this makes her happy. *You need me*, she says to me, every visit, *but you won't admit it*.

"Already?"

I sent her a photo of myself in the ones I'm wearing when I got them at the start of the summer.

"I have headaches."

I take them off and show her how they pinch my temples and the bridge of my nose; they're too small, but they're vintage, and I thought they were cool.

"Those are cute," she says, and makes me put them back on.

She presses one side of the glasses against my ear. "You're sure that's what that is? You're sure it isn't something else? You seem stressed."

I pop an olive into my mouth, look for the pit with my back teeth. "I'm not stressed," I insist, and spit the pit out between my front teeth, depositing it next to the oil-slicked cucumbers on my plate. I think of the dinner table in Brooklyn right now, the beeping of the microwave, my brother-in-law, Dev, cracking jokes, Sacha crawling under the table, food untouched, all the things that Jill calls "a mess" but that I'd happily trade for my mother's unwitting ability to deflate my confidence in my own feelings, that noisy room for this silence that she thinks means she's told me something I don't understand about myself.

My mother's neglected to tell me, until it's just before lunchtime the next day, that she is planning on a one o'clock train home; she and my father are going to a birthday dinner at a neighbor's, and she wants time to decompress beforehand. She leaves me, a new pair of glasses picked out and paid for (we fight over this, the salesman calls us adorable and advises me to listen to her, and it all pleases her), at the lens store.

It's over eighty degrees. My apartment feels dark in the afternoon, and I realize this is the last time I will feel warm sun on my body for a long time. I change into a bikini still optimistically in my underwear drawer, grab a towel, a gift from Jill from a vacation she took a few years ago—Turkey? Jamaica?— that has always seemed so much nicer than something that should be on the ground, and head to the meadow in Central Park. I end up falling asleep, and when I wake and rearrange myself, checking for my phone, my wallet, adjusting the strings of my bikini, where I am surely burning, I meet a man. When I retell this story, to friends, eventually, to Jill, I will leave out the sunbathing part, how I didn't feel naked in front of him, how he barely looked at my body when we spoke. He was looking, I'm sure, before he approached me. He introduced himself using his first and last name, Henry Offerman, lifting his sunglasses to the top of his head as he did this. I told him mine, woozy from the sun, from his simple declarations and questions. He didn't, as all other men do, feed me a line about it. Hope. His smile expanded. He was wearing a suit. I didn't know then that he'd quit his job that morning, that he'd spent the past few hours, as I had, walking around with a kind of stolen freedom.

The suit is nice, but not too nice to sit on the grass in. I offered him a part of my towel, which he accepted. We talked for nearly an hour, as if we planned to meet, as if we already knew each other.

Henry is the first man I've been attracted to whom I've thought of as handsome, my vocabulary for all the men I've been dating in the past few years suddenly inadequate. I'm aware of his age immediately—I know he's older. He reads more like the people I encounter at my sisters' parties: securely employed and married, that side of sure. But he isn't married, and he isn't that much older. Thirty-two, he tells me, a pause before he asks me my age that Sunday, when he takes me out for dinner.

"You seem older," he says to me.

I look for disappointment on his face but it isn't that, nor is it pleasure. Interest, maybe? Relief? Theoretically, I carry less baggage. Theoretically, I'll expect less of him.

"I've always been around adults," I say, feeling like an idiot; I'm an adult myself, have been for some time. "I mean, since I was very little," I add.

It isn't a scandalous age difference. Eight years is less than half of the difference between my own parents, and he's still a good measure from my siblings. It's that he is supposed to be somewhere he isn't yet—married, paired, at least—and I am supposed to be out wilding, shaking off whatever I'm expected to loosen from myself so I don't drag it into my next life.

At dinner, Henry tells me about the job he left, which made him miserable, how doing so made it easy to come up to me that day. "I never would have, on any other one," he says, smiling at the luck of it. He doesn't know what his next move is. He wonders if it's time to go back to Chicago, where he's from, where his family still is.

"Don't," I say, possessed by a boldness I've never had either.

"Okay," he says, locking eyes with me, putting down his fork. "Not yet."

Henry and I leave the restaurant and head out into a crisp evening, though under my dress, the skin on my back is peeling from that afternoon in the sun. At a corner, my reflex to check for a child's hand kicks in and my fingers graze Henry's, on accident, but he looks at me under a light that's already changed, as if I know something he's only just realized. He pivots my body toward his and kisses me right on the edge of the curb, the other pedestrians choosing which side to walk around us. Everything seems possible.

When we say good-bye through the bars next to the subway turnstile, our fingers touching one last time, I wish him a good week, when I mean to say night. The next Sunday, late in the afternoon, he texts to ask if I'm free for dinner. He's just landed at JFK, back from a weekend with his family, a wedding or some such life event that he'd mentioned offhand. I think about my presence at those sorts of things, how half a dozen people must have asked him if he was seeing anyone. Would he have mentioned me? How we met? How many days has he been thinking about me?

He takes the taxi directly to my apartment, whose floors I sweep with a paper towel. I quickly load my dishwasher. I am clean, at least.

His face in my doorway is more than I am ready for it to be, a certain relief at the way he seems to be remembering me, at his slightly stale airplane smell. No one has ever come home to me. I know this isn't what this is, but it's close enough to give me a little ache for it, to let myself imagine a future that's mine.

By December, Jill's news is out, and Henry and I are having dinner every Sunday. Sometimes, in between looking for jobs, he meets me for lunch at my office, or for a movie on a weeknight. The whole time we are dating, Henry goes on interviews, which aren't exactly dates with other women, but sometimes they feel this way, the ones elsewhere—in Washington, D.C., and in Chicago, especially. In these months I learn what he smells like, what he tastes like, the places where he is soft, the sound of him trying not to wake me in the morning, the order in which he puts on his scarf and hat and gloves. When my mother comes to town again, I invent errands so I can talk to him on the phone outside, even though it's cold and we aren't talking about anything that has an endpoint. "I have seven blocks," I'll tell him, and he teases me about how he is my secret.

My parents are going to London for Christmas, to see Jack and his wife and the two girls. They offer me a ticket, casually over dinner one night in Connecticut, where I am for the Thanksgiving weekend (Henry is in Chicago), but I say I want to stay in New York; Henry and I have New Year's plans. I'll go to Jill's for Christmas; the kids are insisting I sleep over. I am vague about New Year's but specific about Christmas. "Oh, that's a great plan," my father says. He's always amused when Jill and I deliver news about one another to him.

"Since when are you two so close?" my mother wants to know.

It's not much of a stretch to picture Jill as I first remember her: young and cool and mischievous. The cigarettes she never finished in time for me to miss noticing when we met her outside somewhere; I can hear my father clucking his tongue, feel the reflexive tightening grip of my mother's hand as we approached.

"I don't know," I say. It seems I can't remember a time when I lived in New York and we weren't, when their house didn't feel like mine in a way the one I'm sitting in now does less and less.

"The free trips will stop after a while, just so you know," she says with a little smirk.

"I know," I say, and try not to roll my eyes.

"Katherine," my father says, half-sharply, half-laughing. He still doesn't know whose side to take.

"I'm teasing," she says, leaning back in her chair with the last of her wine. "London in December isn't much to look at."

"I know," I say again, and ask Dad about work.


On a beautiful afternoon in April, Henry waits for me outside my office building. It's Friday, and my boss is away for the weekend, so I cut out a little early. Henry's sitting, knees spread, sunglasses on, on the edge of a fountain in the plaza outside. When I reach for his hand, he takes it with a sigh, and I think he's just relieved to see me.

"You up for walking a bit?" he asks.

"With you? Always." I kiss his cheek.

He puts his hand on my face. He's not usually up for a lot of contact in public, so it seems, then, especially sweet. It's that kind of day: sunny, not too warm, and my legs are bare, and he smells like a fresh shower and a shave, and I feel, on that Friday afternoon, incredibly lucky, at ease, pretty and smart and on the way to something good, with Henry, with myself.

My phone dings in my pocket, a coworker asking if I want to come to happy hour with them, but I don't reply. I explain to Henry that my phone's on because Jill's labor could start at any time. Both Anjali and Sacha came just past their due dates, and Jill doesn't want this one early, but I am anxious for her to arrive, to do what I'm supposed to when she comes. "Sure, sure," he says, then, "Can we stop?"

He points me to a park—a small triangle, really, the ivy thick in it already, and the bench is in the shade—and I walk through the open gate with him. "You okay?" I ask.

Here's the way he says it: He's moving to Chicago. Not that he's taking a job there, which he is, a good job, one that sounds if not exactly right for him, right enough for now, to let him know what might be right for later. This is one of the things we talked about, one of those mornings in bed when I didn't want to go to work and he had nowhere to be on that day, and the sunlight would get brighter and brighter in my room. He wouldn't tell me not to go, but he'd lay a hand over my thigh, nudge at whatever I was still wearing in bed. In February and March especially, it seemed we couldn't get enough of each other, the last days of dark afternoons that I hoped, then, unlike I had any other winter in my life, would stay longer, so we could give in to bed earlier, so that we'd get quicker to the part of the night where he'd fit a hand under each of my breasts and say into my ear, *You*, and only that, but it was enough. Those mornings were hard, waking up, leaving him. He'd work a finger under the edge of my underwear, or a strap of my tank top, as if considering how responsible he was willing to be for making me late, and we talked about these things, moving and jobs and the future. I believed we were building him, together. I don't remember if he asked me what I wanted. I was too enthralled by what he was doing to me, the way he always gave in, and I'd let him spin out his mind till it was so spent he could focus on my body, and we'd have sex, quickly, but always at his urging, his failure to let me go. That made it all all right: being late for work, how quickly it was over, how it pained me to think of how long it would be till I'd get him again, looking at me that way, talking to me as if I were the insides of his own mind.

The job is one thing. But then, on the bench, his face a shade of red not from the walk, but from shame, he mentions Paige, by name, as though she were a mutual friend. I know Paige. Paige, he almost married. Paige, whom he moved to New York to forget. I'm still holding his hand and not letting him take it away. He begins, at that moment, actually, to stroke my palm with his thumb, but we're both sweaty and clammy at this point, our bodies in various states of panic. Paige is in his mind again. She is in his life again. He still loves her, he's realized. Enough to give it another shot, enough to say it aloud to me.

I still haven't taken back my hand. I'm still holding on.

"Hope," he says, part question, part apology. No one ever knows how to say my name right when they are disappointing me.

The best thing to do would be to let go of his hand, to not ask him to explain, but I need to understand what I've missed. We talk in the park for another hour, quietly, as the sun starts to sink and the day turns flat. When I've heard all that I can, I take the train to my sister's in Brooklyn.

Jill is finally, at this stage, not going out on a Friday night; she opens the door in a dress and no makeup, as radiant as ever. Dev has just come in from work, and gives my arm a squeeze as he loosens his tie. "I'll order us food," he says, and goes upstairs to change. I finally cry in the kitchen, where, on various baby-sitting nights, I've held each of the kids against me as they've wept over grievances that felt ridiculously small: a broken plastic toy, a wrong look from a friend, and more so now.

Jill, a month from her due date, moves as fast as she ever did. The kids are downstairs watching a movie, but she takes me into the pantry, closes one of the two doors, and wraps her arms around me. "I'm sorry this is a shitty hug. There's a giant human in the way."

She gives the impression of being delicate of body and bone—her fine features, her pale coloring—but she is unafraid of risk or person or making a mistake, generous. Her hugs, when given, are like being wrapped in a straitjacket. She doesn't ask me why I'm crying, but what she can do. Still in her grasp, I shrug.

"It's that boy, isn't it?"

"That man," is all I can get out. She opens a fresh box of tissues from a shelf behind her, hands it to me, whole. I tell her what happened in the park.

Jill says to me, "Clearly, he's not good enough for you. He's not ready."

It's the sweetest of lies. He was perfect. I am the girl who made the other girl look like everything, who made him ready for her. I am the one who's not good enough.

Two weeks later, my mother is in town, just for the day. She has an appointment with a lawyer, something about the business she used to own, but she wants to have coffee with me before. She meets me at my building and we take the train together in the direction of my office.

We stand, as we always have, up against the far set of doors. The train is full, but not bad for a morning commute. She rests her hand on the crook of my bent elbow for balance. She squints at my face.

"What?"

"You using a new moisturizer?"

My mother is obsessed with my skin.

I shake my head no. Then I start to cry.

"Why are you crying?" she asks, pursing her lips, wiping a tear from my cheek with her thumb.

"I don't know," I say. I have made it almost three years here without crying in public; leave it up to her to make this happen.

It all comes out then, the whole story of Henry, how we met, how I felt about him, how it's already over.

As I tell it, my mother doesn't look at me—she has never been able to do that when I cry, even as I do so silently, as one does on public transportation. I try to look at her, but my glasses are cloudy with my tears. "Not here," she whispers, adjusting the shoulders on my coat, smoothing my hair. She's out of practice with New York City, the way people use subway cars like holding spaces: putting on makeup, finishing work, sleeping and eating and checking themselves out in the doors as if no one else is watching. We all are; we just pretend not to be. I am but one body in tears on the 1 train. I only mind crying here because my mother is watching me do it.

When we get off the train, she hands me a tissue from her purse.

"You're too young for that, anyway," she says. "You understand?"

I take the tissue and nod my head, though I do not understand. Halfway down the block toward the coffee shop, she stops us mid-walk, turns me to face her. She wipes the last tear from my cheek with a fresh tissue. "Look at that skin, Hope. You have so much time."

When the baby comes, just four days later, it's fast. The children are asleep when I get to Jill and Dev's place, and when they wake up, she's already here. I don't sleep much that night, my phone abuzz with messages and e-mails from phone numbers I don't know, the list of people that Jill gave Dev—in New York and London and Paris and Charlottesville and Ridgefield—waking up to the news, all the parents and the exes and the second spouses and siblings and baby Kiri's rosebud lips. I feel tears come into my nose as I show Anjali and Sacha the photos of their new sister, the phone vibrating in my hand with each congratulations, each declaration of her perfection.

"Do we have to go to school?" Sacha asks.

"Why are you crying?" Anjali wants to know, their questions crossing.

"Sometimes people cry when they're happy," I say, and then, "Yes, we do," though I'm not sure if happiness is why I'm crying today, why this baby is making me cry. I saw the look on Jill's face, her preemptive exhaustion, as she kissed *me* as she left for the hospital under Dev's arm. It wasn't joy, exactly, but I know it's what I want.

"Where's the blood?" Anjali asks, skating her thumb and pointer finger across the screen to make Kiri's picture larger.

"She's all cleaned up there," I say.

"Aw," she says, frowning. "I wanted to see the blood."

Sacha asks for breakfast.

I get the kids to their schools and myself back to bed; it's not worth it for me to go to work, and the weekend is ahead of me, full of all those people coming in, kids to bring back and forth to the hospital, the playground, the diner three blocks away for the umpteenth grilled cheese and undercooked french fries. *My sister had her baby*, I text Henry before I can change my mind, or think about why I want him to know. He's in Chicago by now, his apartment, his life in New York emptied and over in a matter of weeks. He'd asked that I stay in touch. He'd apologized. I turn my phone off and go to sleep for a few hours.

I wake up just after noon in Anjali's bed. Dev's left a voice mail, asking if I wouldn't mind getting Jill some pajamas; she didn't, for this baby, prepack a bag, and had forgotten them. He assumes I know where they are, and I do. I have spent so much time in Jill's closet that I only open a few wrong drawers before I find the right one. I find, too, a tote bag to put them in. On top of the bureau in the closet are framed photographs: the kids when they were babies, dirty with ice cream or jam on their rounded cheeks; Jill and Dev on their honeymoon, standing on some island cliff, a big sun hat on Jill's head; and the one of Emily and my father, that though I've seen it many times, I always do a double-take on. The frame on that one, a mosaic of warm orange and peach tiles, is heavy when I lift it; I've never been able to really get a good look at it with Jill there—not that she'd mind, or question my curiosity, but I am still shy in this, in things concerning Emily. The frame is missing a few tiles from the corner, as though it's been dropped. I know this used to be in the living room, collected on the bookshelves with all the other markers of time, though I never saw it there; it was before Jill and I were close—who knows, maybe it was before I was here at all. "It upset Caitlin so I moved it," Jill explained, with a face, the first time I noticed the photo. She was putting together a bag of clothes for me, yanking things from the hangers seemingly at random and folding them swiftly into a stack before I could say if I wanted them. This was two years ago, right after I had graduated college, right after I'd moved back to New York. I'd asked her who that was in the photo, and then, before she could reply, asked, "Oh my God, is that Dad?"

She laughed, said, "I know, right?" and kept pulling, folding, stacking.

It's no secret that my father and Emily were unhappy from the start. Jill claims this is the only photograph of them smiling together. They do appear genuinely pleased with each other, with themselves. They're in T-shirts, but over bathing suits; you can see a red string tied at the back of Emily's neck. Her hair, blond, wispy, just like Caitlin's, in a high ponytail, the wind on the beach blowing a still-wet strand to the left. My father's eyes are bright and he's leaning his head toward hers, and she is receiving it. They're looking at the camera, the both of them, but in a way, they're looking at each other; they're seeing themselves together, their possibility. No one can remember or agree when or where it was taken: Montauk? Laguna Beach? On the sound? Was Jill born yet? Jack? Were they married, even? It's not my place to ask if anyone has asked.

Today, on the floor of Jill's closet, in a life that mine won't resemble, I'm grateful that this photo exists, for the story of this moment of Emily and my father, and all of us who follow, grateful that Jill is wise enough to keep it, to believe in this story, even if she has to hide it from the others. I know it's there. She's shown it to me, the place where I can find it.

It's me and the kids in the late afternoon at the hospital when my father arrives from a meeting he had in the city. He kisses us, washes his hands, and demands the baby, whom Jill has swaddled and stretched out on the length of her thighs. Dad takes Kiri, pulling off her hat so he can see her hair, which swirls, jet-black, along the back of her head. I'm happy to see this coloring, her father's, her siblings', because it brings her closer to me, makes the team of brunettes stronger than the team of blondes on my half siblings' sides. "Never gets old," Dad says as he walks the small perimeter of the room with Kiri in the crook of his arm, muttering alternately to her and to us. He smiles, he coos; he looks like a pro, and he is: He's holding the tenth baby in his genetic line. The three of us—Jill, Devdan, and I—are worn out, but my father is energized by this little empire of his ego. He's so sure that she is right, that we are right.

I leave the hospital with my father. We're both headed uptown, and I offer to ride with him toward Grand Central. "If you'd like to," he says, but I know tonight he's delighted by us, by me, by naming me correctly. I know he wants my company.

On the subway, my father takes his tie off, folding it into an accordion shape and holding it in the same hand as he does his briefcase. It's been a while since we've been on the subway together. For a couple of years, when my mother was working late a lot (some promotion she'd gained or was trying to), he'd leave his office early and pick me up from after-school two days a week. He always looked out of sorts entering the cafeteria, where we all dumped our backpacks and jackets. Part of this was his exceptional height; I knew by then, the fourth grade, that I, too, would be taller than the other kids, and this perspective always caused both of us to survey our surroundings as though we were responsible for something that others couldn't see. Years later, I imagined this look was in part because he felt worn out by still doing this kind of thing, twenty-plus years after he'd started, Caitlin by then out of the house at college, and me, still with all that time to go—but maybe he was just looking for me in the crowd of kids.

He always got me earlier than my mom did, and once I gathered up what I needed, he'd touch my shoulder and guide me to the subway wordlessly. We were both done for the day, and he'd fold up his tie like he does now. By that hour, I was too tired to take my backpack off, but he'd ease it off my shoulders and into the space between my feet on the floor so I'd have more room to lean back. He'd always take a seat across from me, not next to me. We wouldn't talk, and any person would think we were strangers, if not for the slope of my nose, the outline of my chin. We don't talk today, either. After we see my half siblings, I never know what to say that won't open up a gorge, or drag us into the ones we know are already there. He falls asleep. He always does. He has three stops before I'll need to wake him.

We hit a station with cellular service and my phone buzzes in my pocket. Henry: *Sweet.*

The first time I teased out for Henry the whole mess of them, the family tree, from Emily down to then-unnamed Kiri, the brief summary of who left whom and who fought and how and the ways in which we worked, or didn't, some years, he wanted to know if I was "like them."

"Which ones?" I asked.

He lined the heel of his hand up against mine. My fingers are long, too, and my hand was barely short of his.

"Which family?" I asked, and my own question caught

something in my throat. I worked my fingers through his, squeezed.

"Hey," he said. "I'm sorry."

"I'm not upset," I said.

In my family, someone is always saying, *That's not how I remember it,* and it's become a joke, how many versions of the stories there are, how no one can leave any story alone till it's mangled and full of contradictions and maybe, by then, seemingly invented entirely. I remember after one big family dinner—looking down the length of the folding tables Jill and Dev had strung together for the meal, Jack in town, next to me, jet-lagged but in a good mood, and Caitlin shifting her son, still so little then, not yet talking or walking, from one knee to the other, my parents in the other room with the other kids—when it seemed like my sisters might come to some boiling point over a story like this. I don't remember what the story was, or whom it belonged to to begin with, just that the story involved me, and I didn't want to chime in, to say that I, too, remembered it a different way. It seemed, then, too big a risk, when I still felt lucky enough to be sitting there. It ended with Caitlin throwing the baby's wet burp cloth in Jill's direction, with laughter, with a new joke born, one of us, always now, saying, *That's not how I remember it,* no need to go on.

## Acknowledgments

T his book is nearly two decades in the making, and the list of those who have supported me through that time reflects how many others are necessary on the path to a first book.

My agent, Julie Barer, has been a dream. Thank you for your enthusiasm, your quick reach for reason, and your fierce protection of my art. Thank you to Nicole Cunningham and all the awesome women who power up the Book Group.

My editor, Sarah Stein, had me at hello. What a pleasure it's been. Thank you to Shannon Kelly and the team at Penguin Books for your professionalism and patience during my first go-round.

The seeds for funding for this book began with the Hopwood Awards while at the MFA program at the University of Michigan. The Northern Manhattan Arts Alliance gave me multiple grants in my early days of taking myself seriously, and I'm grateful for those checks, and for the community of artists in Inwood and Washington Heights that NoMAA continues to champion. A grant from the New York Foundation for the Arts kept me afloat and focused in the final stages of writing these stories.

I'm so grateful for the editors who said yes and first published these stories in literary magazines: Laurence Goldstein at *Michigan Quarterly Review*; Junot Díaz and Deborah Chasman at *Boston Review*; David Daley at *FiveChapters*; Linda Swanson-Davies and Susan Burmeister-Brown at *Glimmer Train*; Morgan Beatty at *People Holding*; Peter Kispert, then at *Indiana Review*; Steven Schwartz at *Colorado Review*; Joanna Luloff at *Copper Nickel* (and V. V. Ganeshananthan for pointing me that way); Emily Nemens at *The Southern Review*.

My teachers, who each taught me something different, and who collectively pushed me out on my own boat: Susan Sherman, who somehow got *The Lover* into my fifteen-year-old hands and changed my life. Dan Chaon, who showed me that the heat was in the stories that already belonged to me. Tom Jenks and Carol Edgarian, who taught me to get there sooner. My cohort at the University of Michigan MFA program and its exceptional faculty: Michael Byers, Peter Ho Davies, Laura Kasischke, Julie Orringer, and especially Eileen Pollack, who never spared me the truth, even when I didn't want to hear it.

I rely on the following readers to make my work smarter and fuller. These stories wouldn't be what they are without Neela Banerjee, Christina McCarroll, Mika Perrine, Jackie Reitzes, Brittani Sonnenberg, and Anne Stameshkin. Thank you to KC Trommer, my head postmistress, for our conversations in song and works of art and words. My sanity is intact because of Jes Haberli and Celeste Ng, who are always there with a doughnut or a match when I need it. Pings.

All of these women are formidable writers in their own rights, and the time they have lent to the work of others doesn't go unnoticed. These are the women who have had faith in me when I haven't had it myself. They hold me up.

So many friends have been longtime champions of my work. Priscilla Morales, for her decades of understanding my authentic self, and for her helpful reads. Lizzi Sofge, for giving me more family when I thought I had plenty already. Brian Herrick, pal. You were the first to hold me accountable to my art, and your commitment to making yours continues to inspire me. Sasha Schwartz and the crew at Scribble Art Workshop, for making my kids artists, and for reminding me that art is joy but it's also work. A special thank-you to Natasha Hesketh, whose story about her painting, "Unknown Date," unlocked a key detail in "Second-Chance Family" for me.

There are at least a hundred other women who have shared their stories with me and listened to mine, and I am grateful for our tradition of storytelling as our means of trying to see and help each other. Keep talking. Don't ever shut up.

My dogs Louie (RIP) and Otis provided companionship and needed walks on working days. I promise there are more dogs in the next book.

To New York City, for raising me up, spitting me out, and taking me back in when I realized there was no other place I could belong.

When people ask me how I am able to write, it's because of my parents, Ellie and Jay Lazarin, not only for their loving care of my children (equal in dollars at least to this book's advance), but for never thinking I should do anything else, and whose insistence that I be beholden to what I wanted came at cost to them. Your patience with me as a human and as a writer is the foundation of this book.

My sisters, Sunan Jones and Lauren Lazarin: it is no accident that this book is full of sisters, in all our complications and strengths. I wouldn't want to tell a different story.

My extended family, for all the occasions we've gathered around tables and shared stories and meals and questions.

My daughters, Phoebe and Talia, unwilling participants in the great experiment of motherhood. Thank you for making my life more beautifully messy.

Last, a gigantic thank-you to my husband, Alex Shulman, who has never minded when I disappear with my imaginary friends or my real ones. You've given me the space and time and resources to do the work that keeps me grounded, and I'm grateful for your unwavering commitment to my work and our family, and for always seeing where the two intertwine.